D1094276

HIT IT!

by Michael Hardcastle

illustrated by Bob Moulder

colors by Hye Won Yi

Librarian Reviewer
Chris Kreie
Media Specialist, Eden Prairie Schools, MN
MS in Information Media, St. Cloud State University, MN

Reading Consultant
Mary Evenson
Middle School Teacher, Edina Public Schools, MN
MA in Education, University of Minnesota, MN

STONE ARCH BOOKS
Minneapolis   San Diego

First published in the United States in 2006
by Stone Arch Books,
151 Good Counsel Drive, P.O. Box 669,
Mankato, Minnesota 56002.

Originally published in Great Britain in 2001
by A & C Black Publishers Ltd.

Text copyright © 2001 Michael Hardcastle
Interior illustrations copyright © 2001 Bob Moulder
Cover illustration copyright © 2001 Mike Adams

Library of Congress Cataloging-in-Publication Data
Hardcastle, Michael.
    Hit It! / by Michael Hardcastle; illustrated by Bob Moulder.
    p. cm. — (Graphic Quest)
    ISBN-13: 978-1-59889-027-3 (hardcover)
    ISBN-10: 1-59889-027-1 (hardcover)
    1. Graphic novels. I. Moulder, Bob. II. Title. III. Series.
PN6727.H375H58 2006
741.5—dc22   2005026595

Summary: Scott and Kel are rivals on the same soccer team, the Aces. As they compete
to be the team's top scorer, their team chases after the league championship. Scott and
Kel need to decide what's more important, their personal goals or teamwork.

1 2 3 4 5 6 11 10 09 08 07 06

Printed in the United States of America.

TABLE OF CONTENTS

CHAPTER ONE

Leaning left and then right, sharply twisting right again and then left, Scott cut into the penalty area. As he avoided one opponent after another, the ball remained completely under his control.

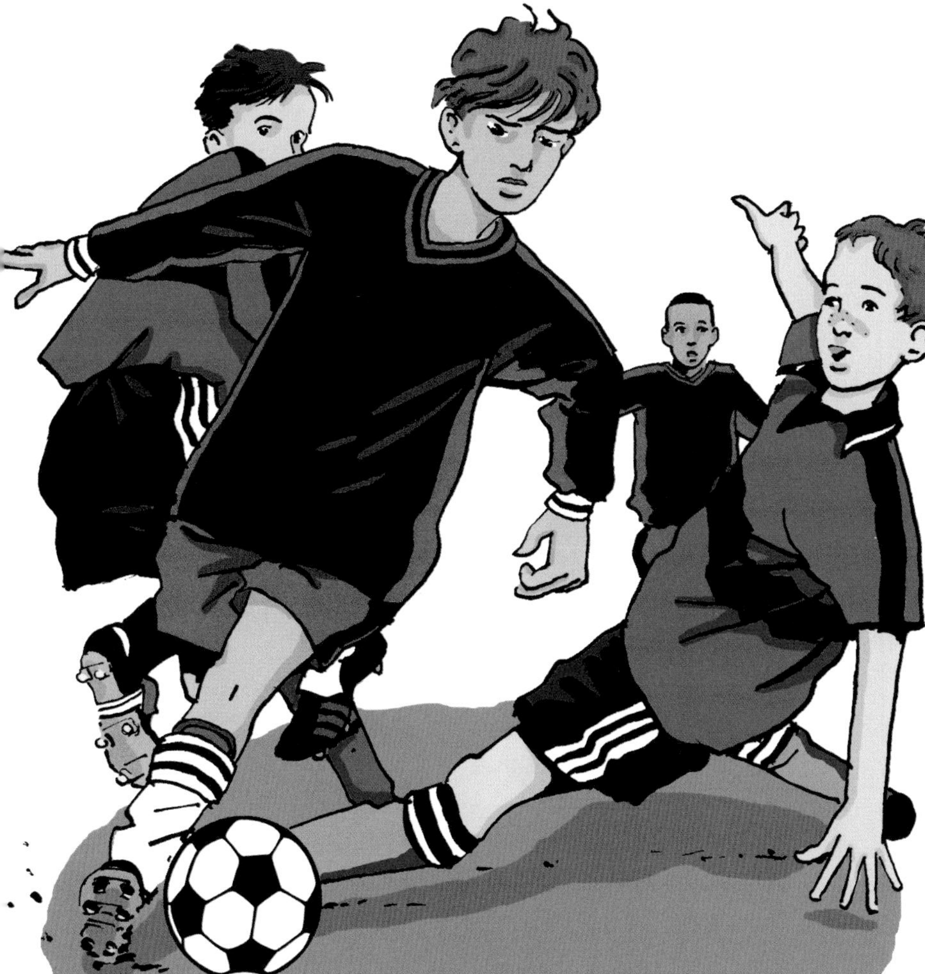

He was sure he was going to score the goal that would move the Aces up in the league standings.

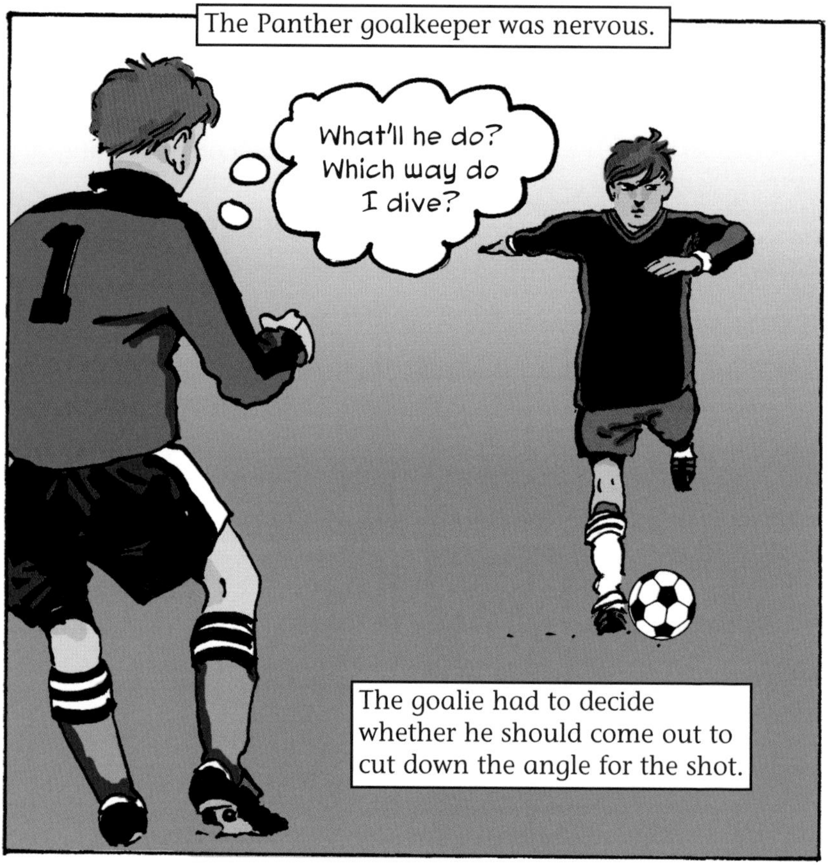
The Panther goalkeeper was nervous.
What'll he do? Which way do I dive?
The goalie had to decide whether he should come out to cut down the angle for the shot.

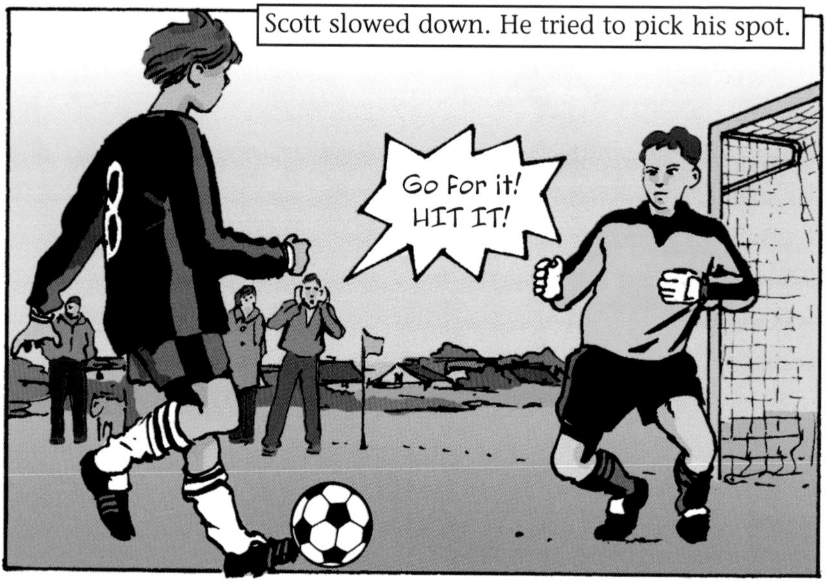
Scott slowed down. He tried to pick his spot.
Go for it! HIT IT!

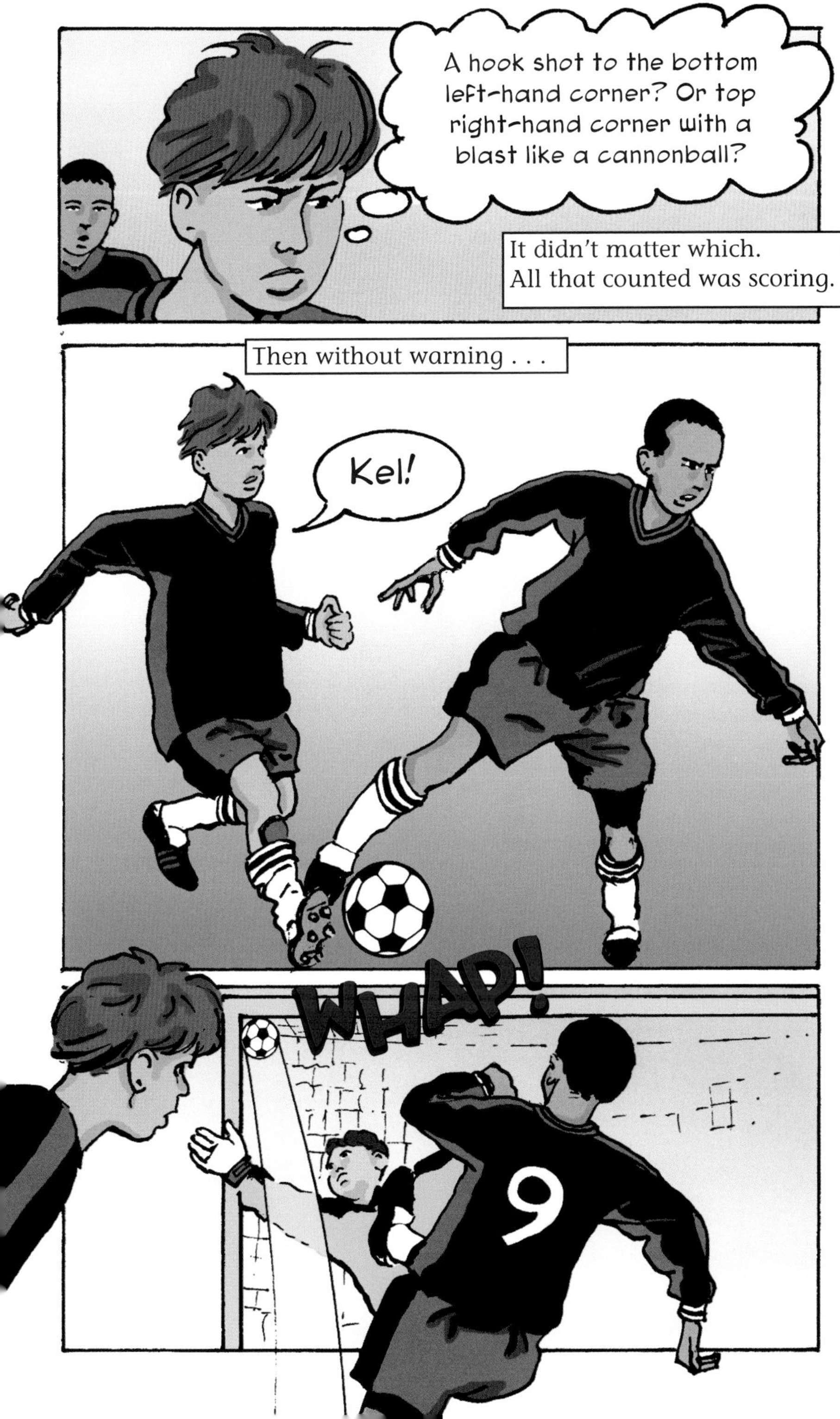
A hook shot to the bottom left-hand corner? Or top right-hand corner with a blast like a cannonball?
It didn't matter which. All that counted was scoring.
Then without warning . . .
Kel!
WHAP!
9

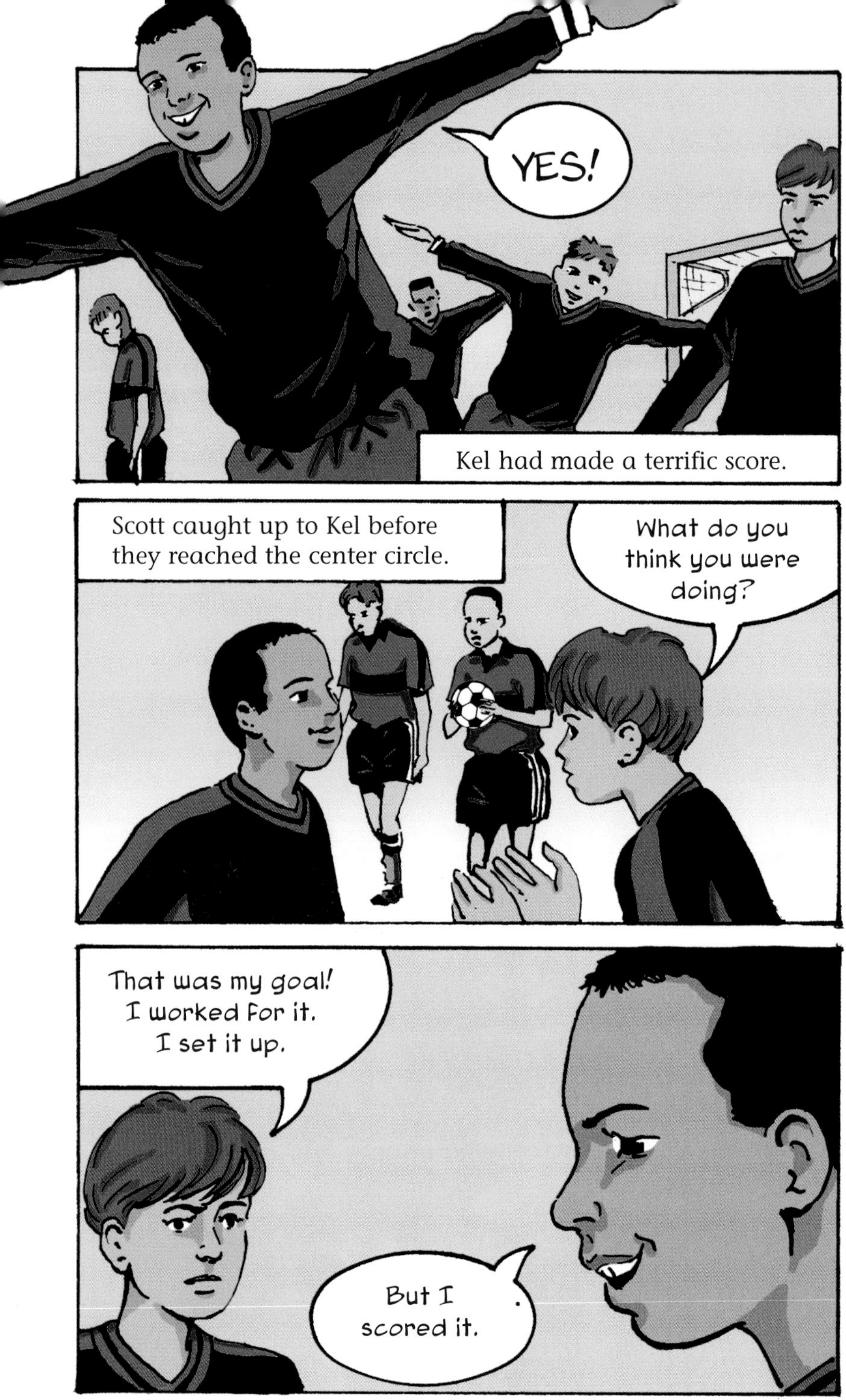
YES!
Kel had made a terrific score.
Scott caught up to Kel before they reached the center circle.
What do you think you were doing?
That was my goal! I worked for it. I set it up.
But I scored it.

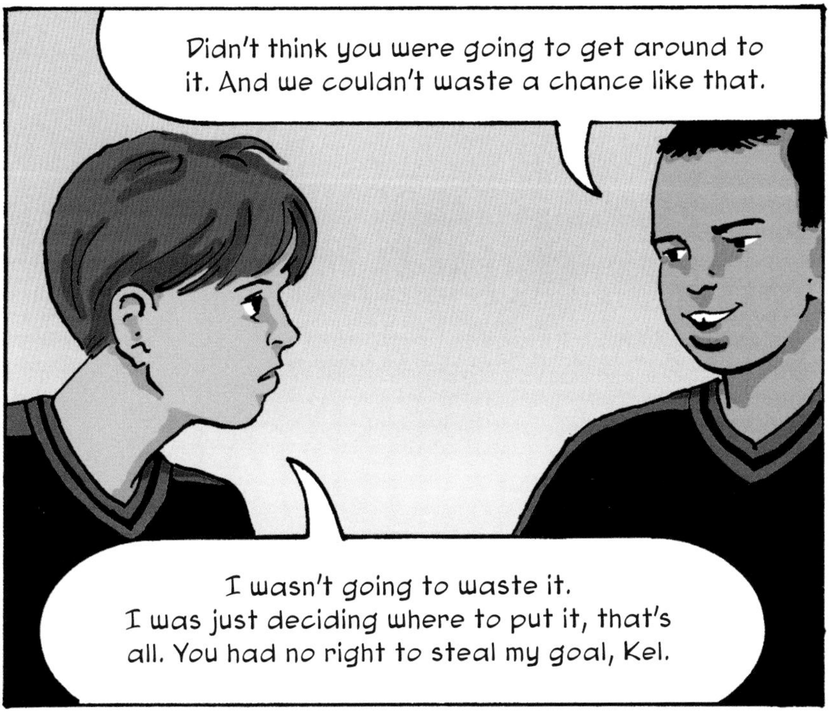
Didn't think you were going to get around to it. And we couldn't waste a chance like that.
I wasn't going to waste it. I was just deciding where to put it, that's all. You had no right to steal my goal, Kel.

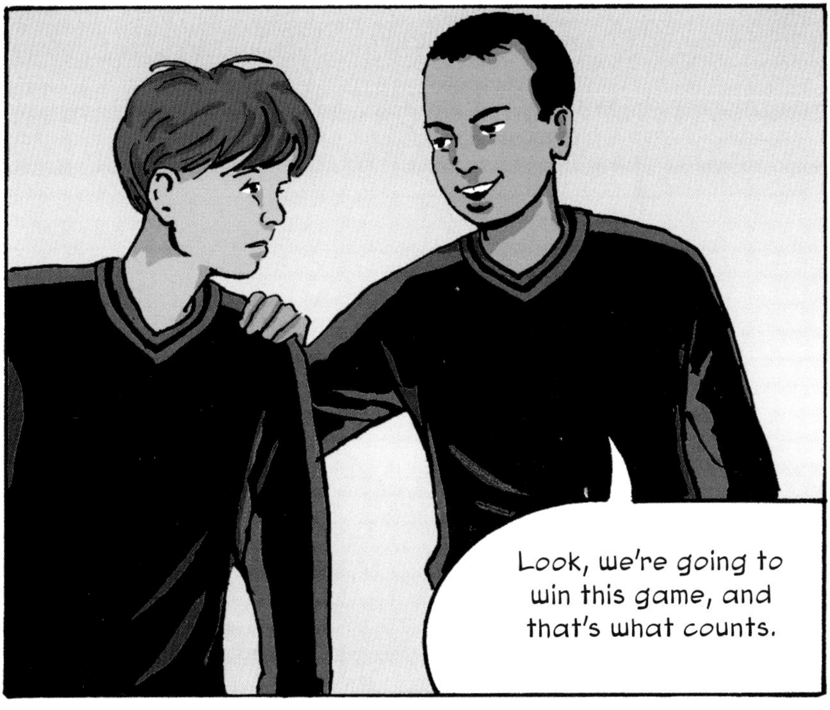
Look, we're going to win this game, and that's what counts.

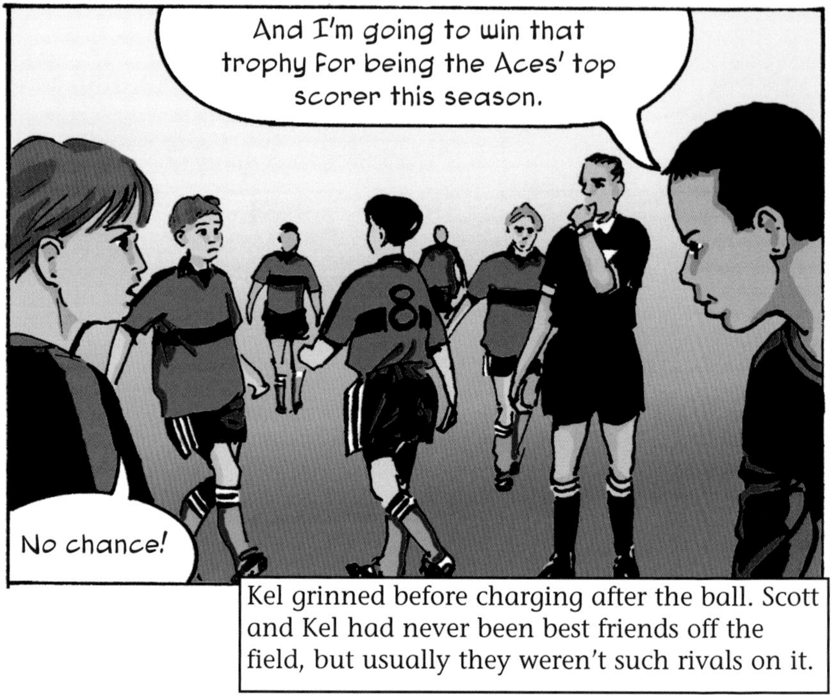
And I'm going to win that trophy for being the Aces' top scorer this season.
No chance!
Kel grinned before charging after the ball. Scott and Kel had never been best friends off the field, but usually they weren't such rivals on it.

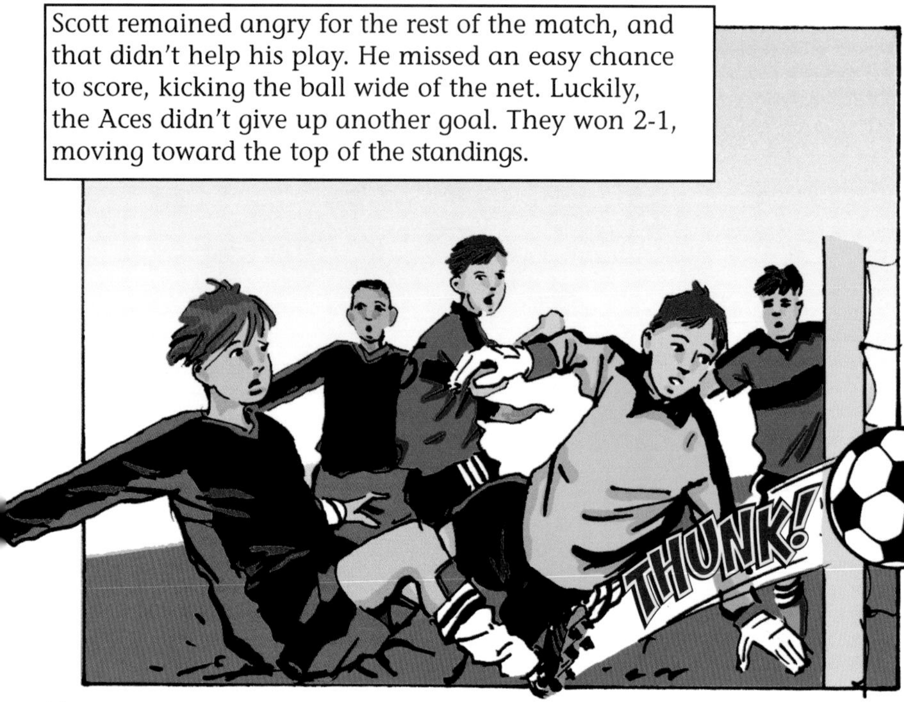
Scott remained angry for the rest of the match, and that didn't help his play. He missed an easy chance to score, kicking the ball wide of the net. Luckily, the Aces didn't give up another goal. They won 2-1, moving toward the top of the standings.
THUNK!

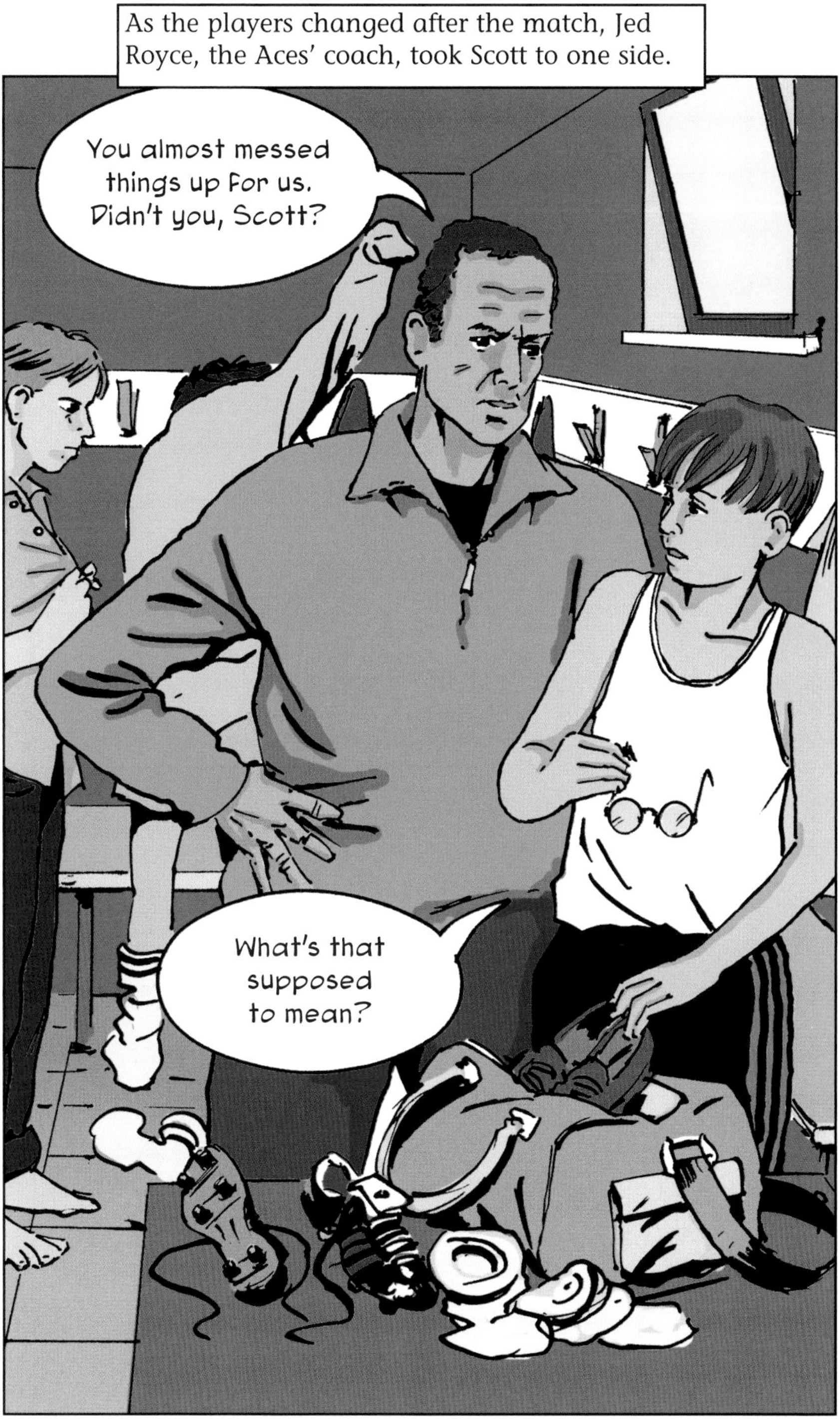
As the players changed after the match, Jed Royce, the Aces' coach, took Scott to one side.
You almost messed things up for us. Didn't you, Scott?
What's that supposed to mean?

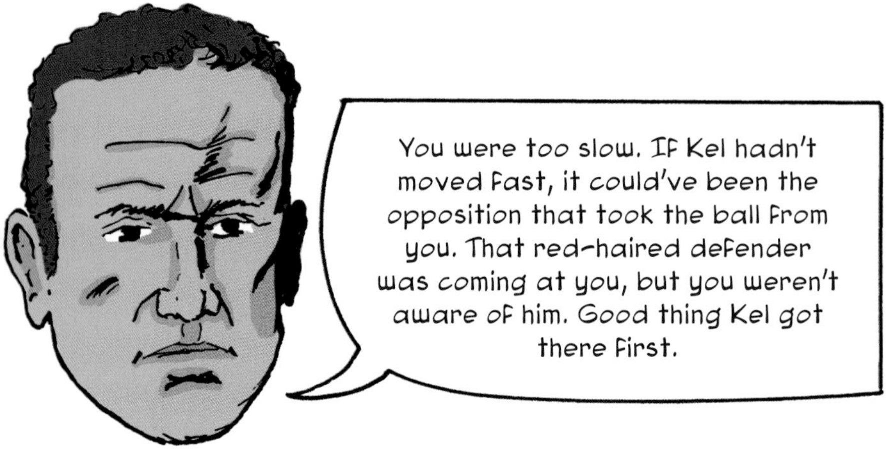
You were too slow. If Kel hadn't moved fast, it could've been the opposition that took the ball from you. That red-haired defender was coming at you, but you weren't aware of him. Good thing Kel got there first.

Scott knew there was no point in arguing. The coach never really listened to any of his players. His own point of view was the only one that mattered to him.

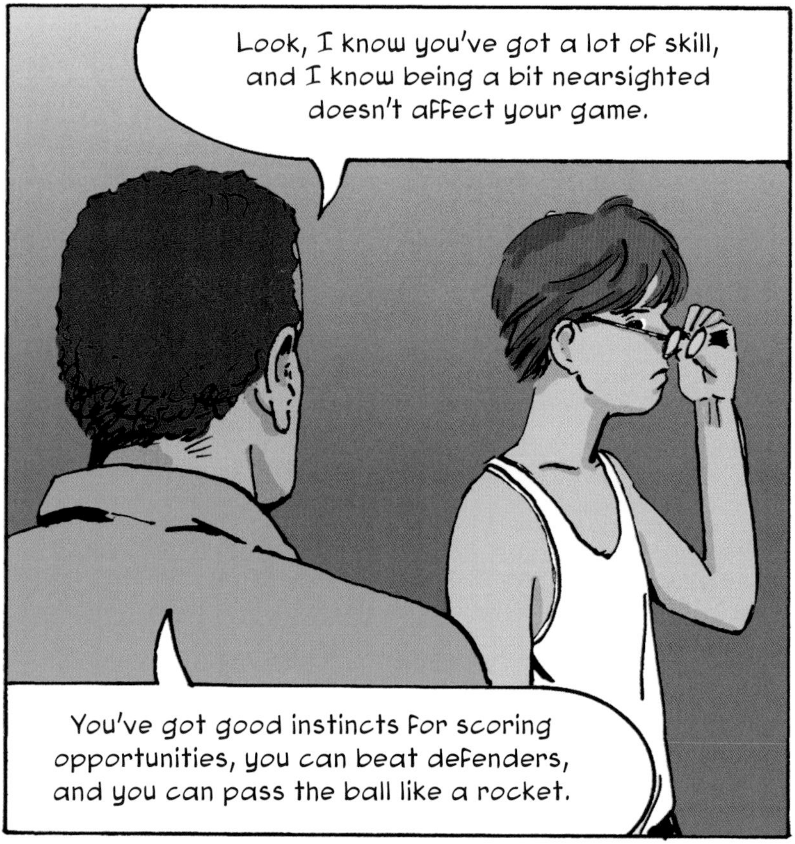
Look, I know you've got a lot of skill, and I know being a bit nearsighted doesn't affect your game.
You've got good instincts for scoring opportunities, you can beat defenders, and you can pass the ball like a rocket.

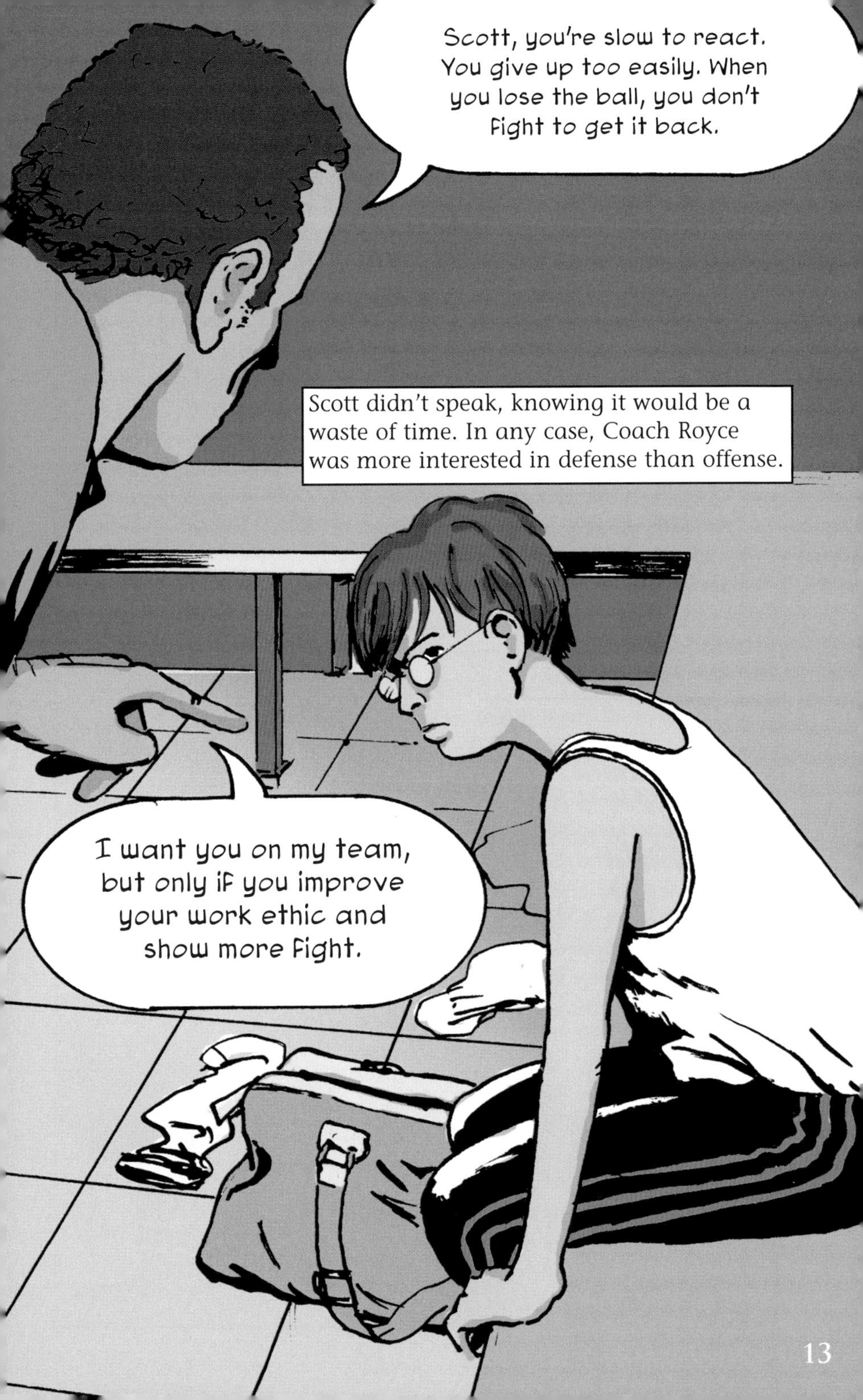
Scott, you're slow to react. You give up too easily. When you lose the ball, you don't fight to get it back.
Scott didn't speak, knowing it would be a waste of time. In any case, Coach Royce was more interested in defense than offense.
I want you on my team, but only if you improve your work ethic and show more fight.

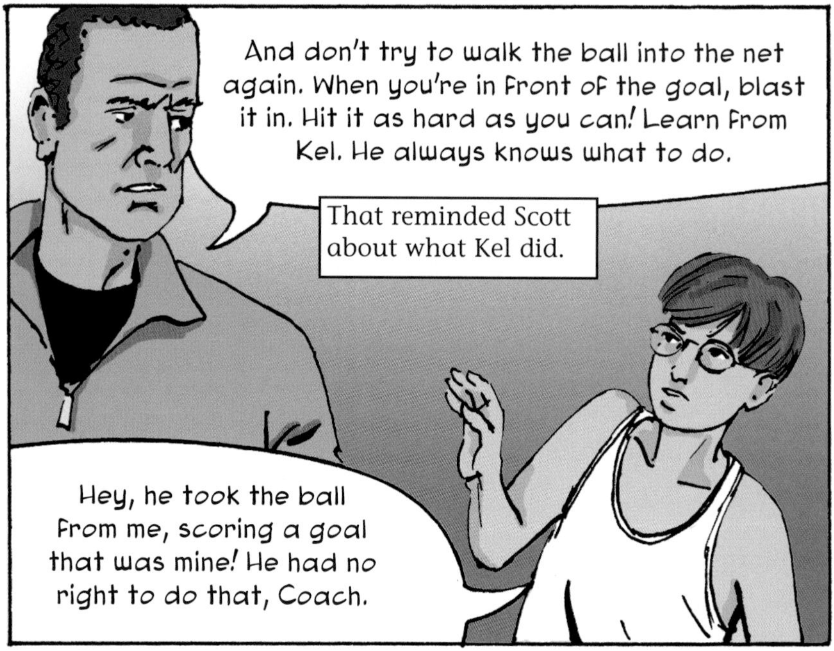
And don't try to walk the ball into the net again. When you're in front of the goal, blast it in. Hit it as hard as you can! Learn from Kel. He always knows what to do.
That reminded Scott about what Kel did.
Hey, he took the ball from me, scoring a goal that was mine! He had no right to do that, Coach.

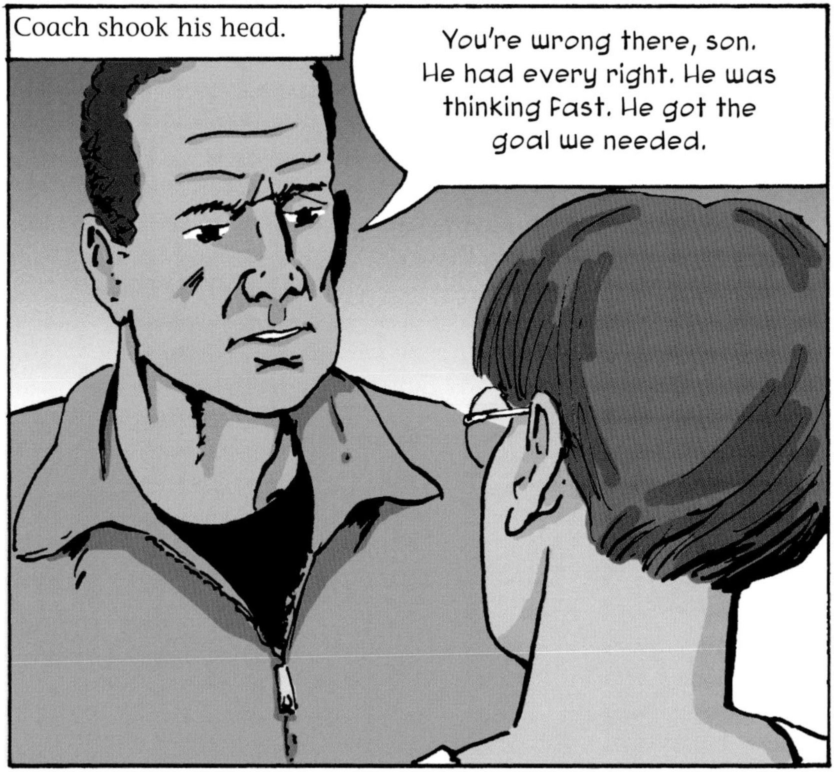
Coach shook his head.
You're wrong there, son. He had every right. He was thinking fast. He got the goal we needed.

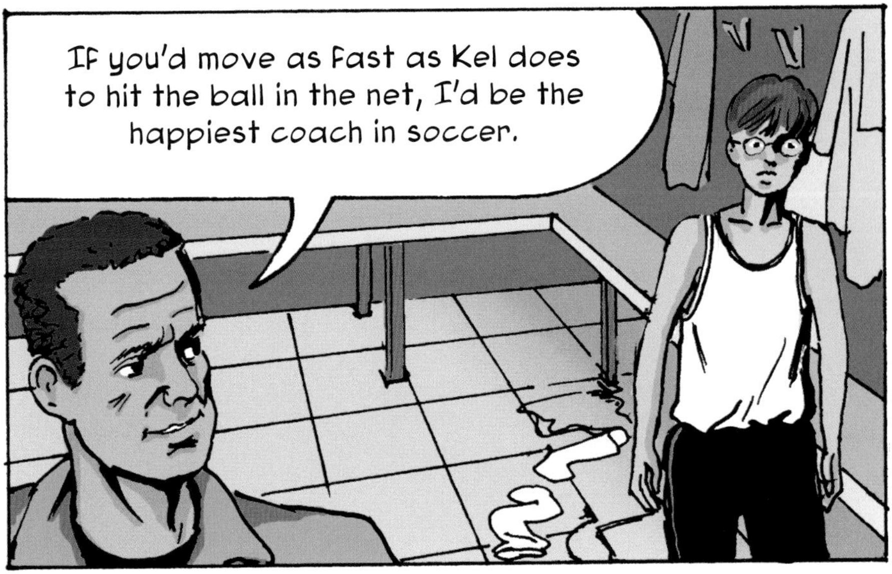
If you'd move as fast as Kel does to hit the ball in the net, I'd be the happiest coach in soccer.

For the rest of the day, Scott's family couldn't get a word out of him. All Scott could think about was Coach Royce's remarks. He wondered whether he would soon be off the team. The Aces were the best thing in his life. If he didn't play for them, he'd feel terrible.

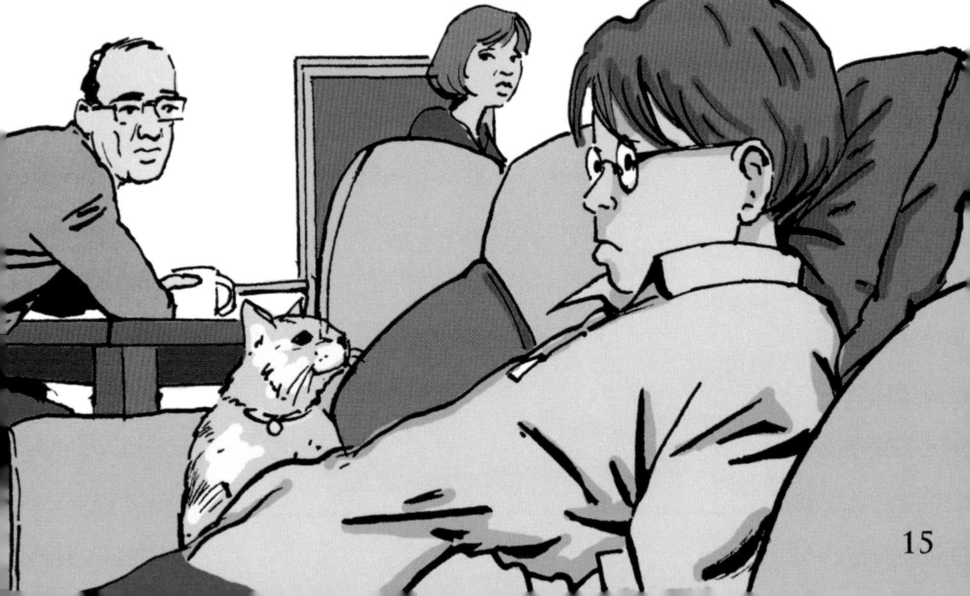

CHAPTER TWO

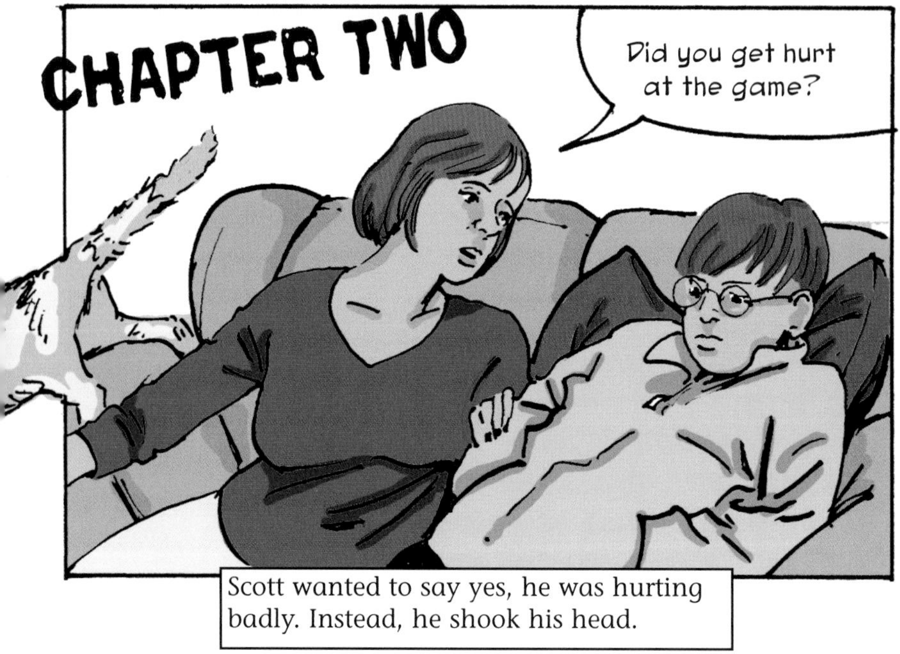
Did you get hurt at the game?
Scott wanted to say yes, he was hurting badly. Instead, he shook his head.

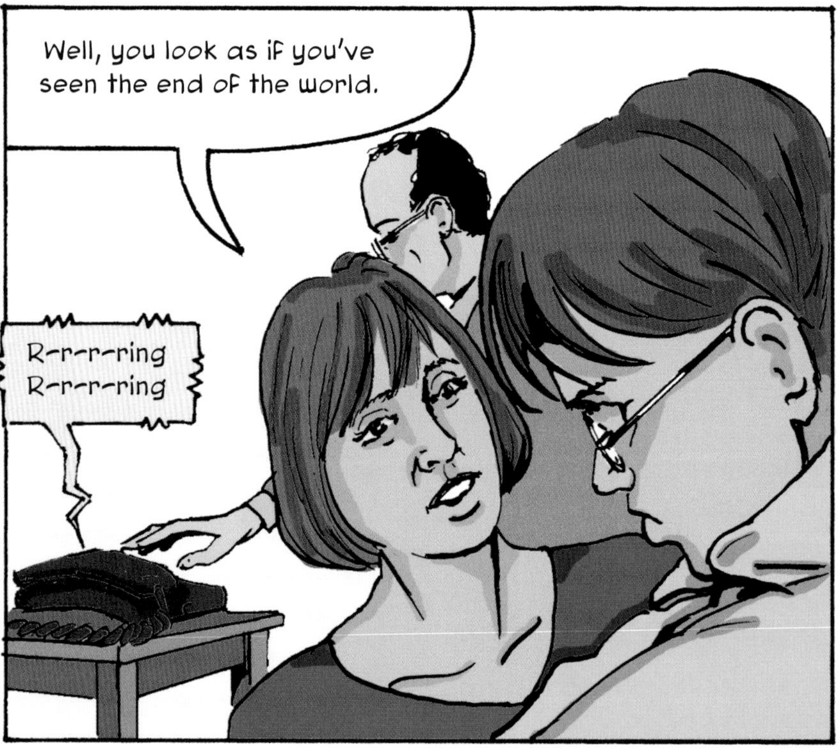
Well, you look as if you've seen the end of the world.
R-r-r-ring R-r-r-ring

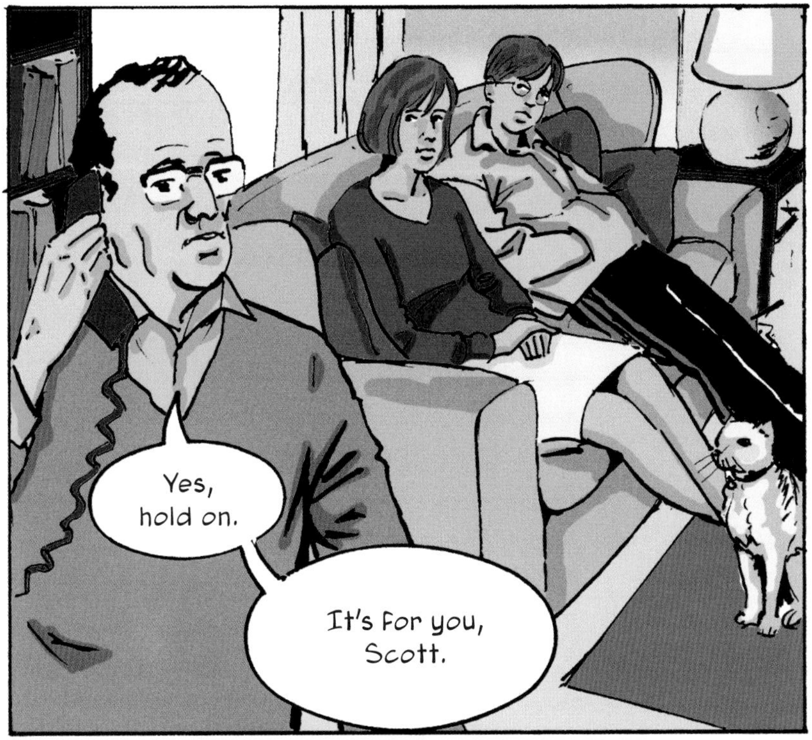
Yes, hold on.
It's for you, Scott.

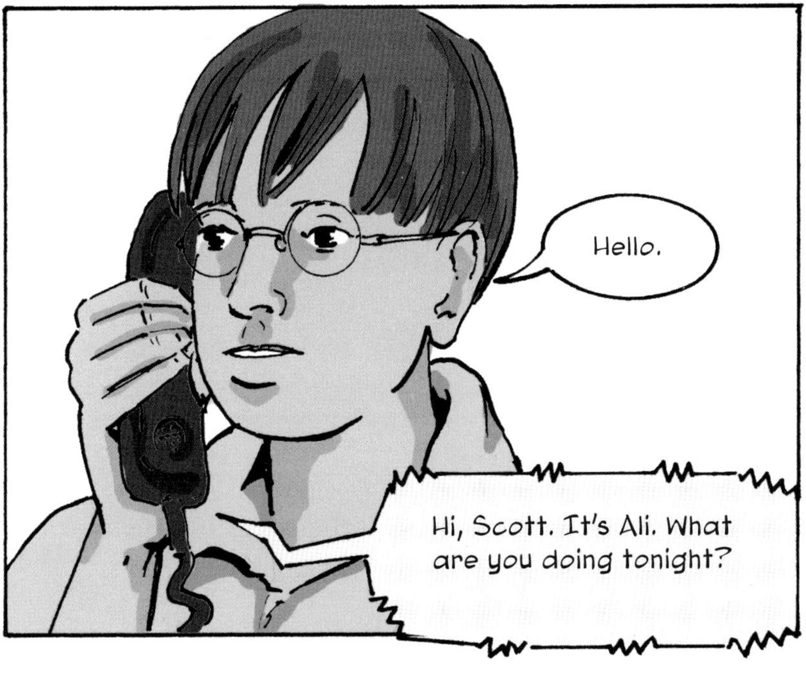
Hello.
Hi, Scott. It's Ali. What are you doing tonight?

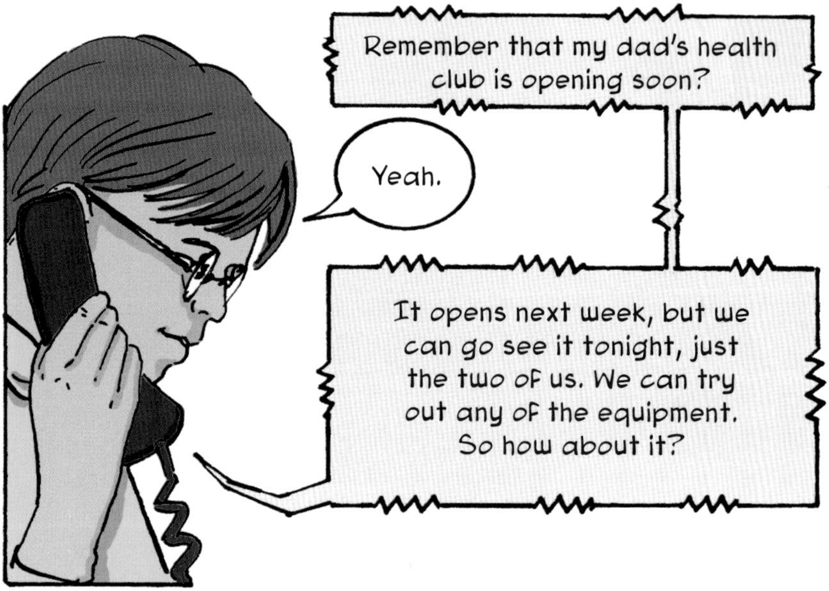
Remember that my dad's health club is opening soon?
Yeah.
It opens next week, but we can go see it tonight, just the two of us. We can try out any of the equipment. So how about it?

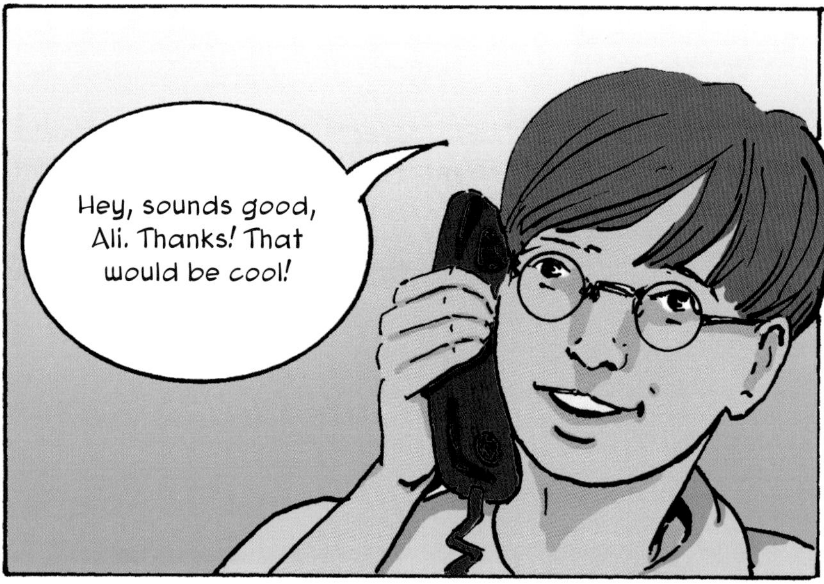
Hey, sounds good, Ali. Thanks! That would be cool!

Ali's father had just retired from boxing. Running the health club was his new career. Scott had never been inside a health club, so he was eager to see what it was like.

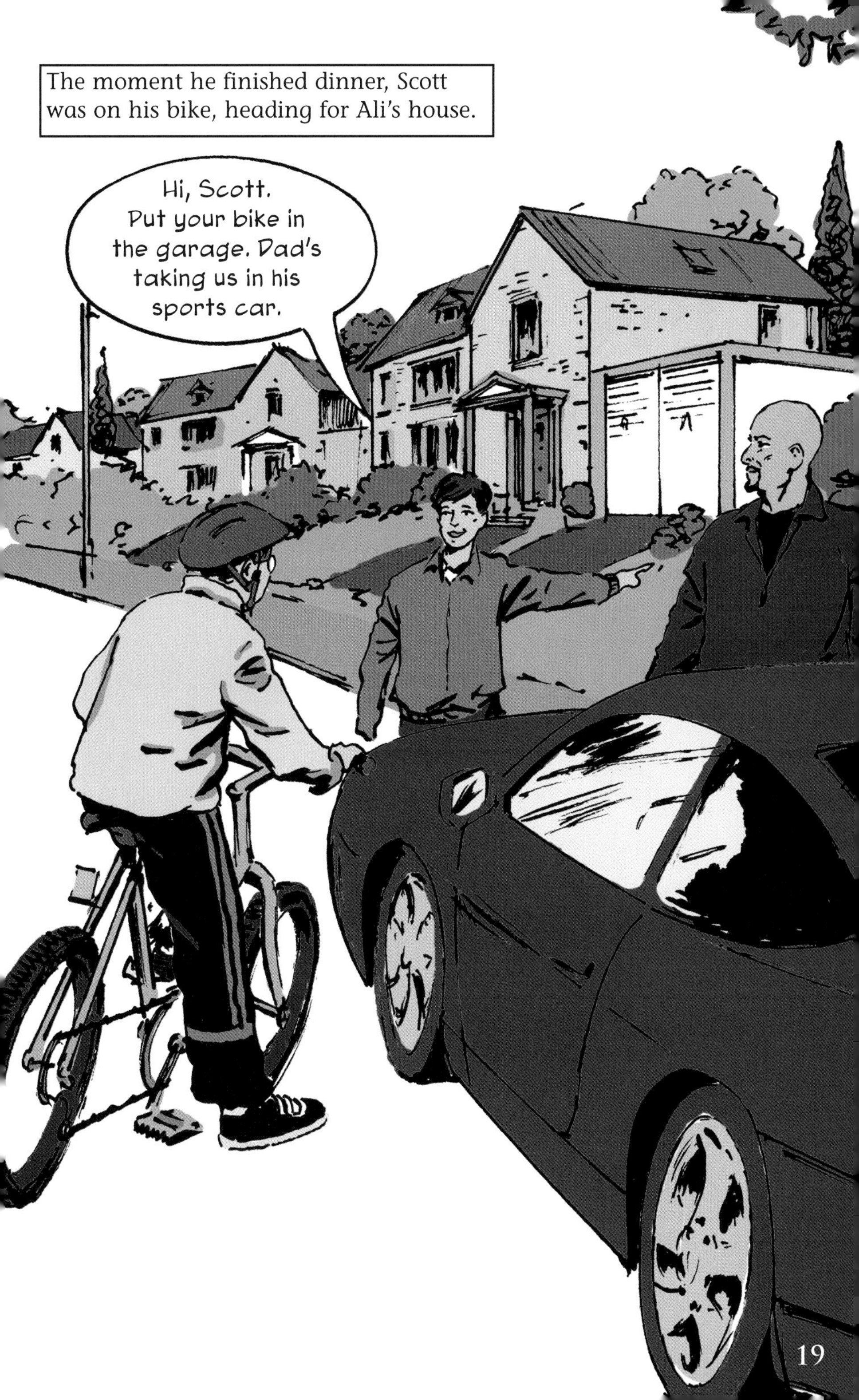
The moment he finished dinner, Scott was on his bike, heading for Ali's house.
Hi, Scott. Put your bike in the garage. Dad's taking us in his sports car.

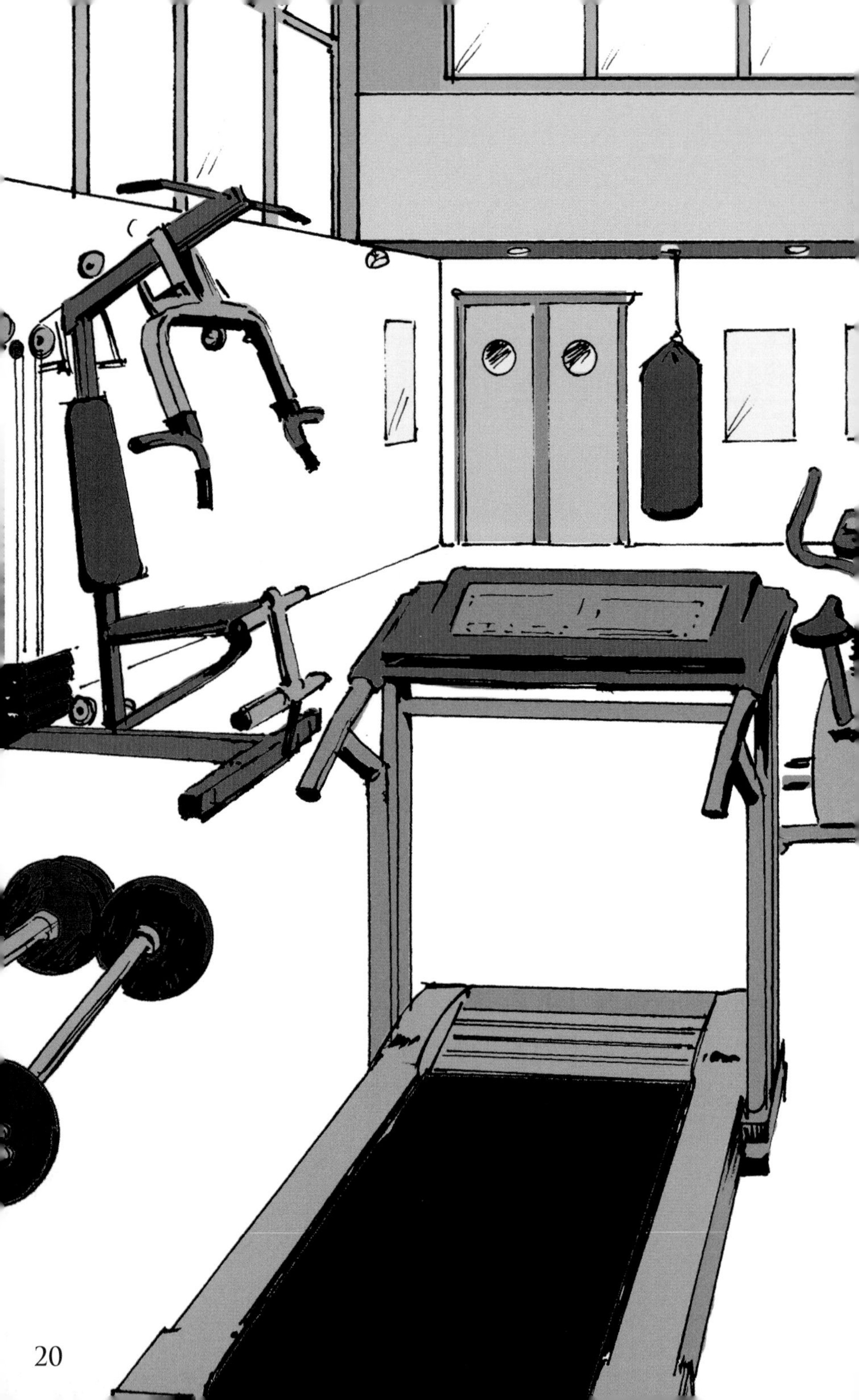

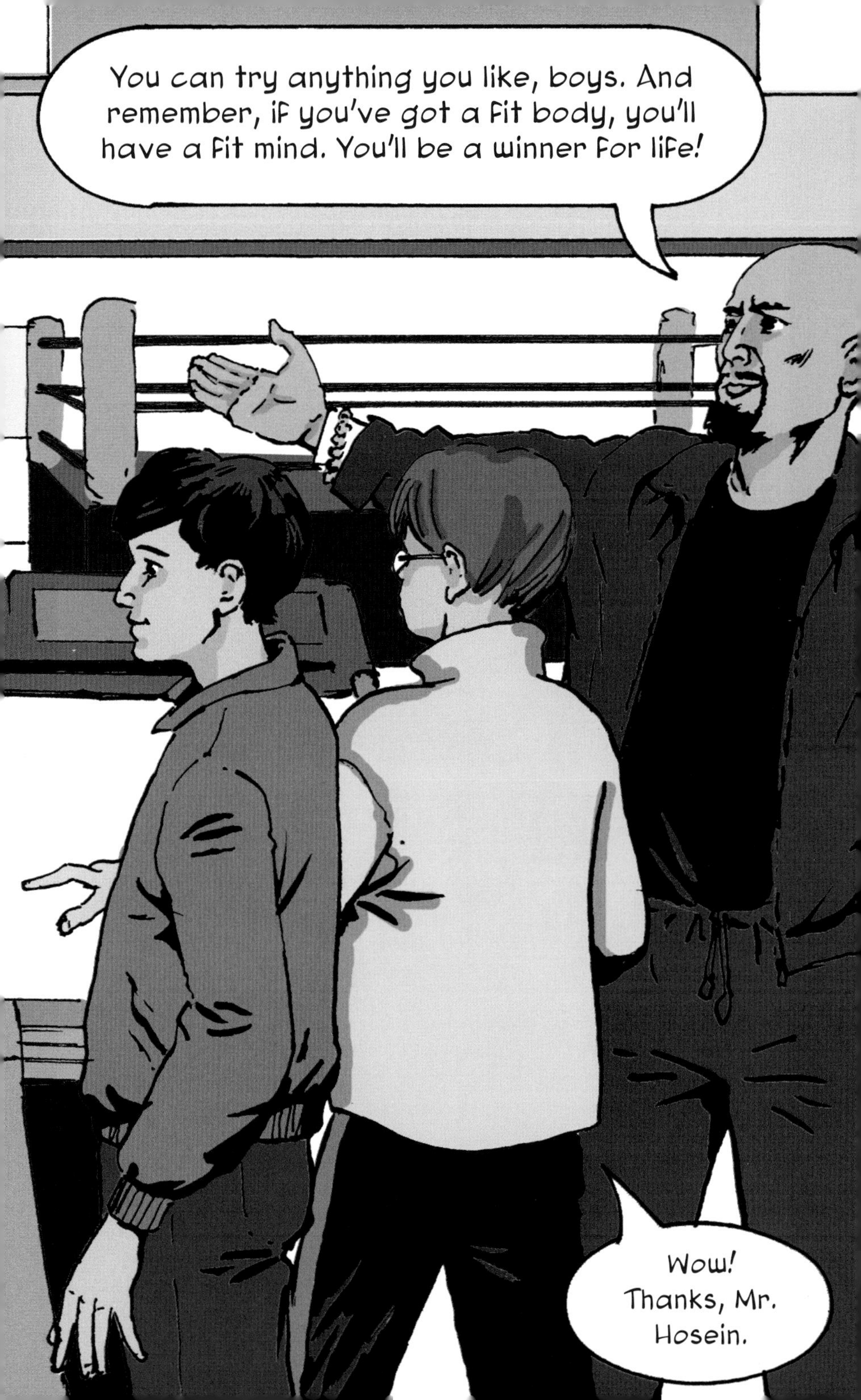
You can try anything you like, boys. And remember, if you've got a fit body, you'll have a fit mind. You'll be a winner for life!
Wow! Thanks, Mr. Hosein.

On the walls were posters advertising the fights that Harri Hosein had fought. He'd been a champion in his division.

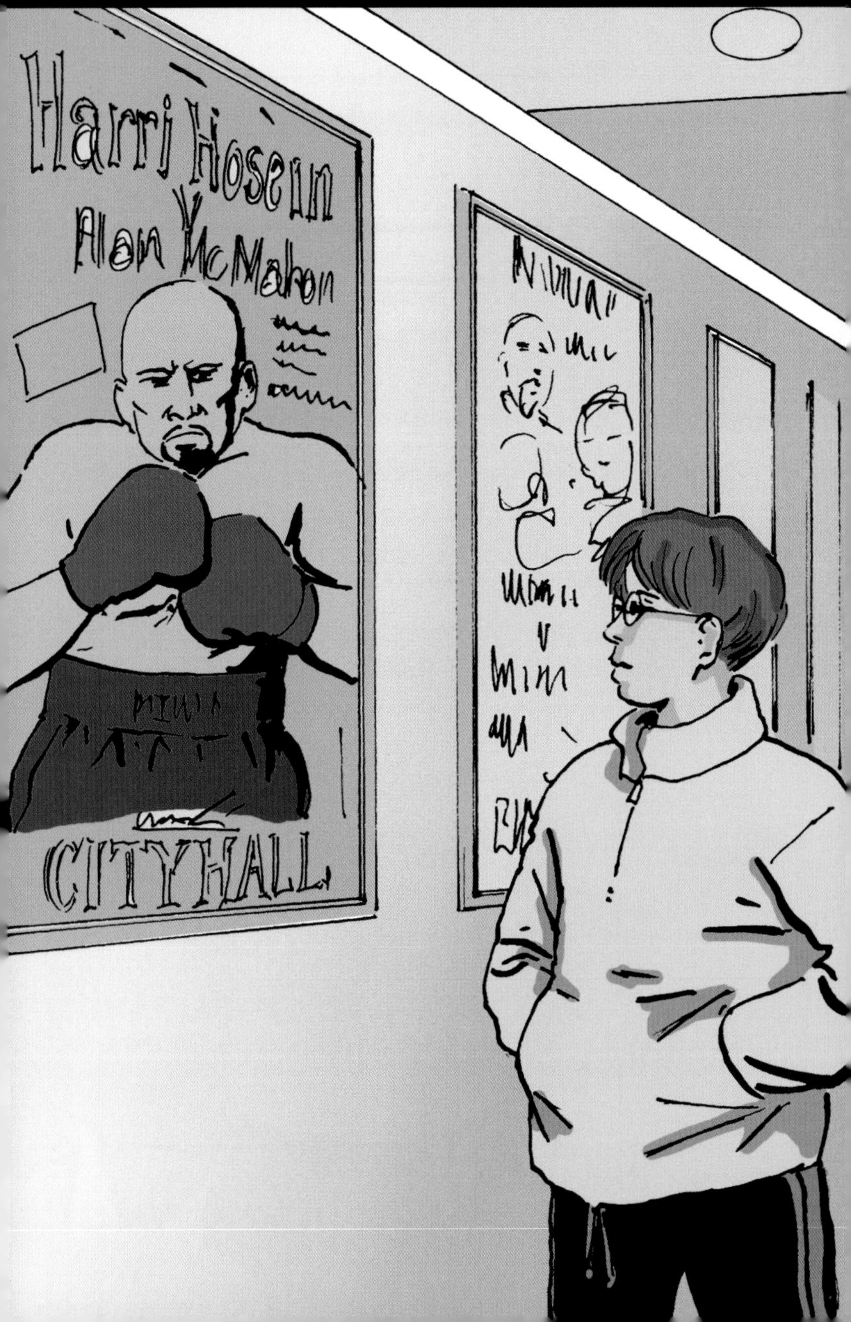
Harri Hosein
v
Alan McMahon
CITYHALL

One in particular caught Scott's attention.

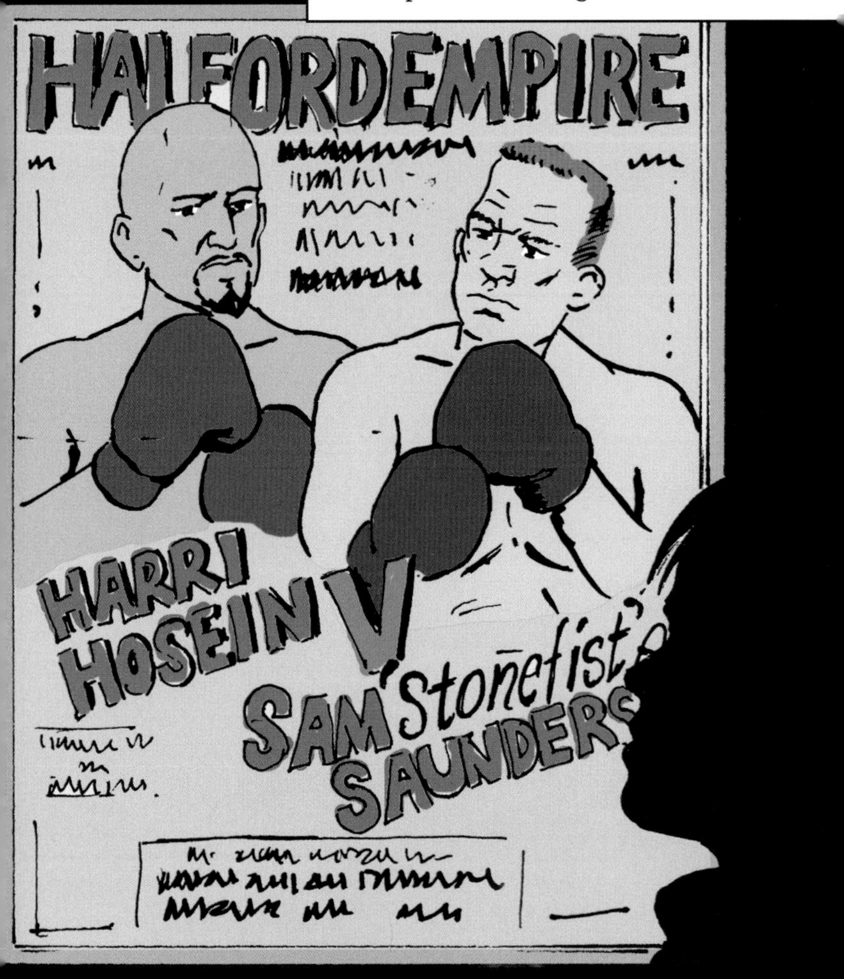
HALFORD EMPIRE
HARRI HOSEIN V
SAM 'Stonefist' SAUNDERS

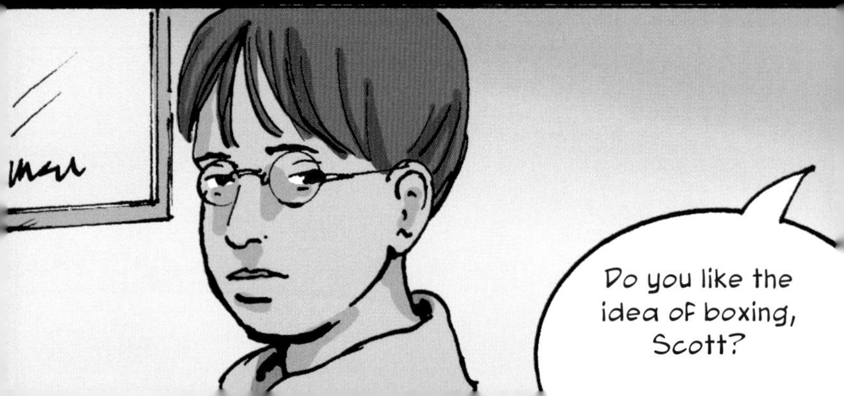
Do you like the idea of boxing, Scott?

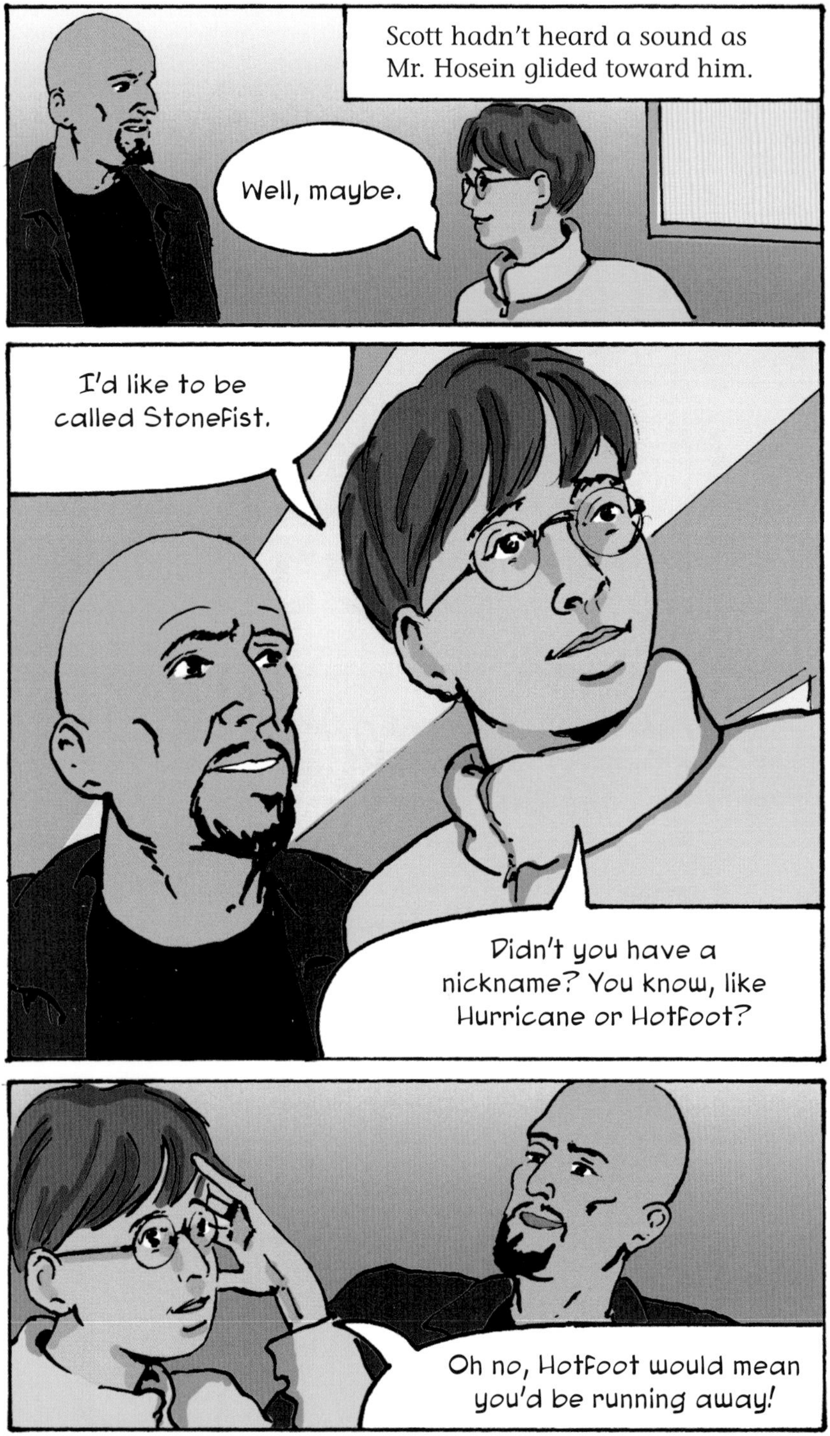
Scott hadn't heard a sound as Mr. Hosein glided toward him.
Well, maybe.
Didn't you have a nickname? You know, like Hurricane or Hotfoot?
I'd like to be called Stonefist.
Oh no, Hotfoot would mean you'd be running away!

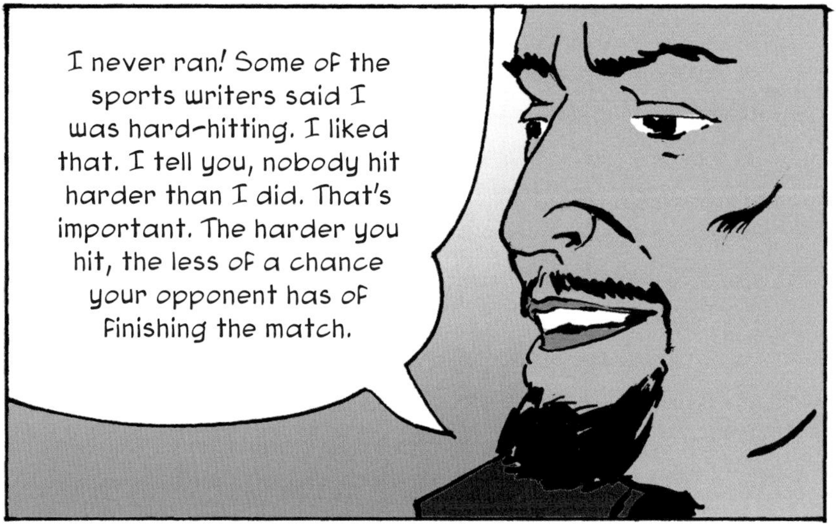
I never ran! Some of the sports writers said I was hard-hitting. I liked that. I tell you, nobody hit harder than I did. That's important. The harder you hit, the less of a chance your opponent has of finishing the match.

Scott blinked. This was the second piece of advice he'd been given in a few hours about the value of hitting hard.

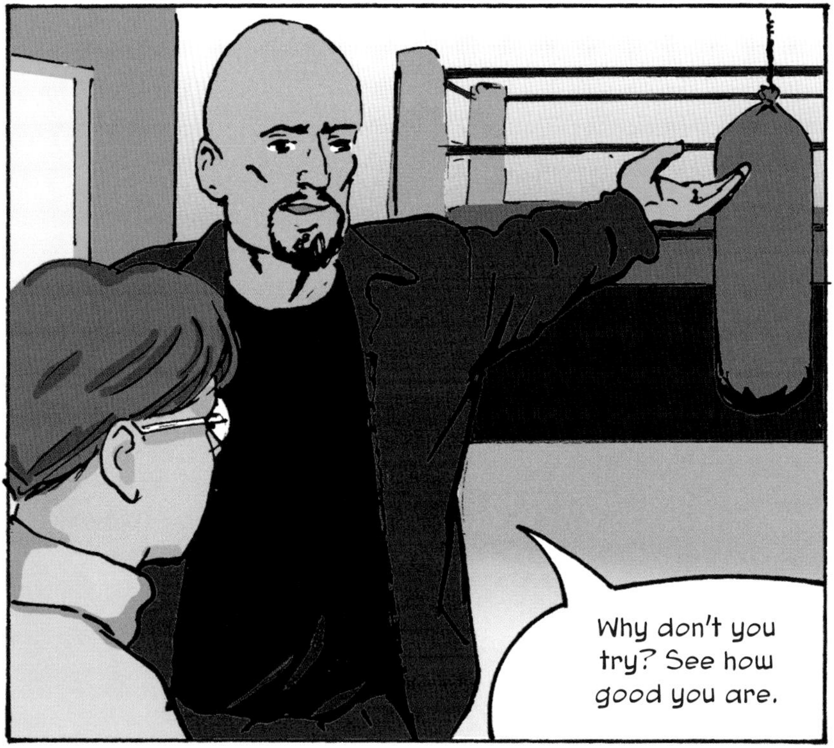
Why don't you try? See how good you are.

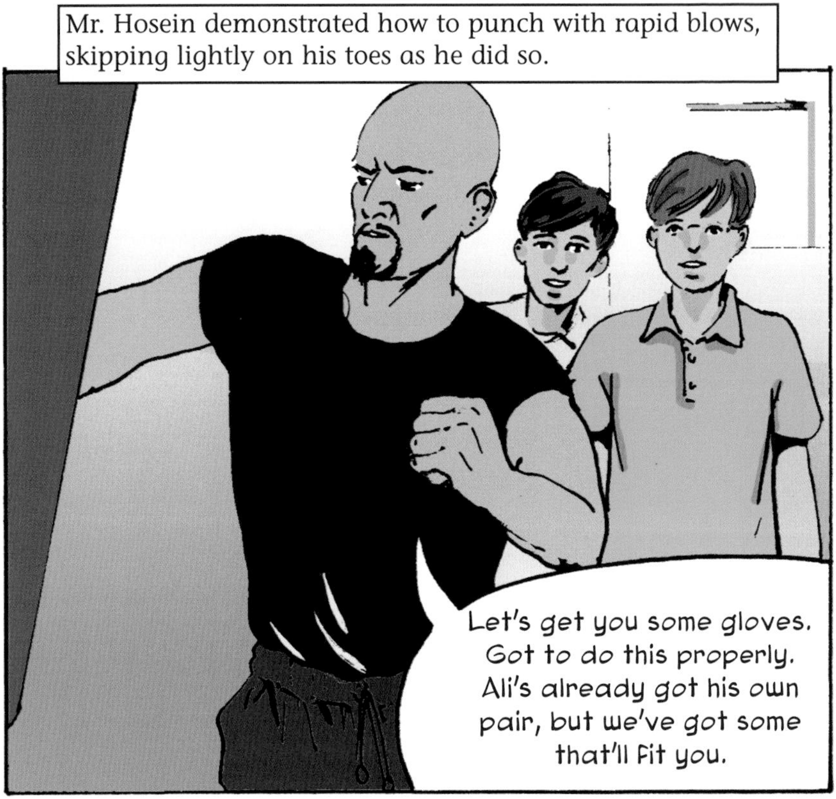
Mr. Hosein demonstrated how to punch with rapid blows, skipping lightly on his toes as he did so.
Let's get you some gloves. Got to do this properly. Ali's already got his own pair, but we've got some that'll fit you.

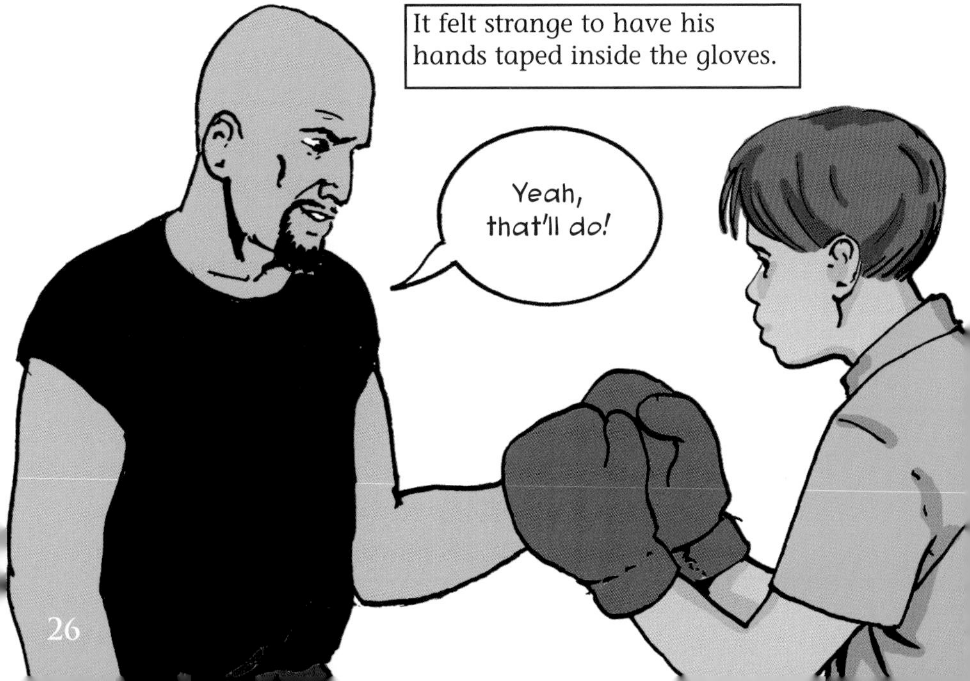
It felt strange to have his hands taped inside the gloves.
Yeah, that'll do!

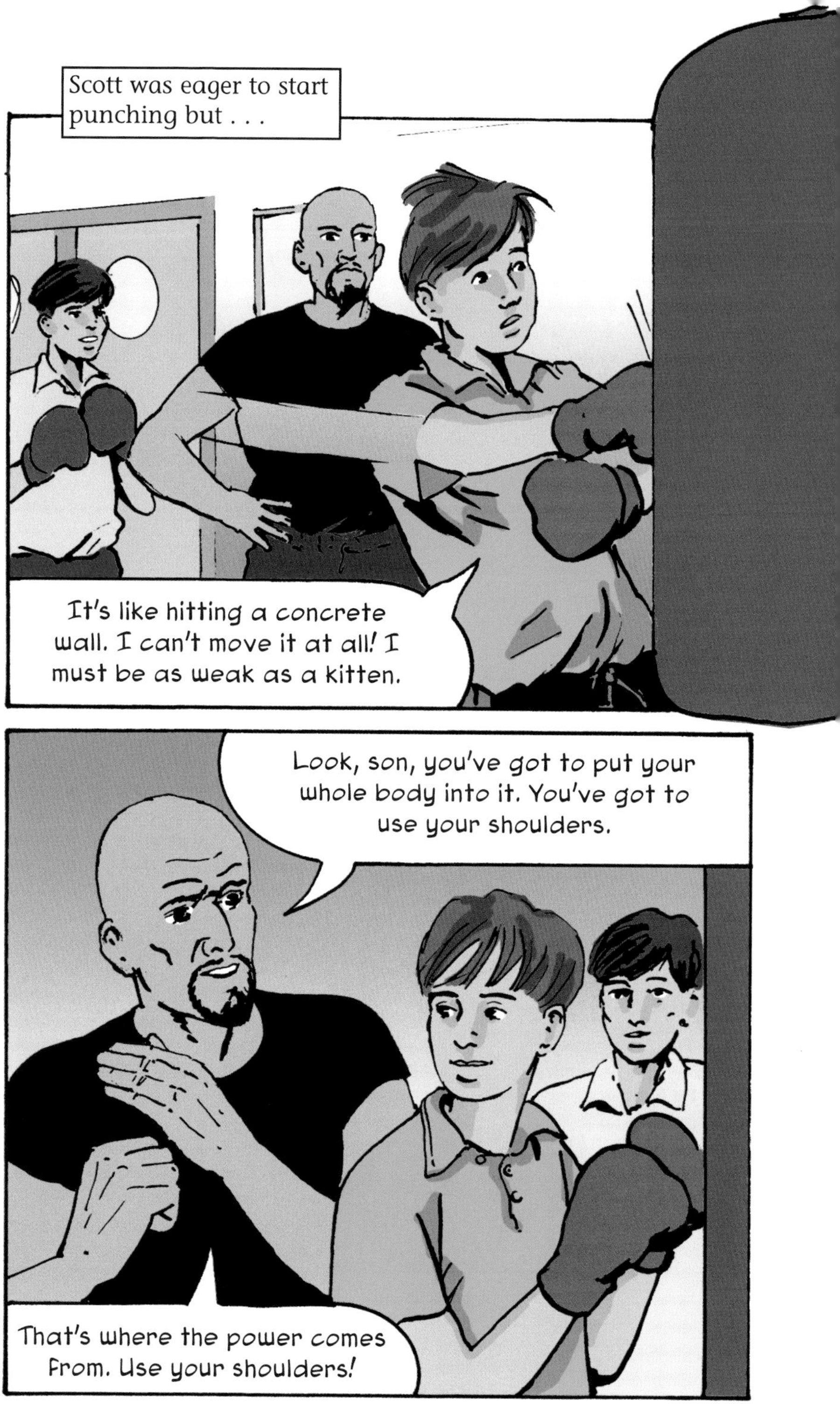
Scott was eager to start punching but . . .
It's like hitting a concrete wall. I can't move it at all! I must be as weak as a kitten.
Look, son, you've got to put your whole body into it. You've got to use your shoulders.
That's where the power comes from. Use your shoulders!

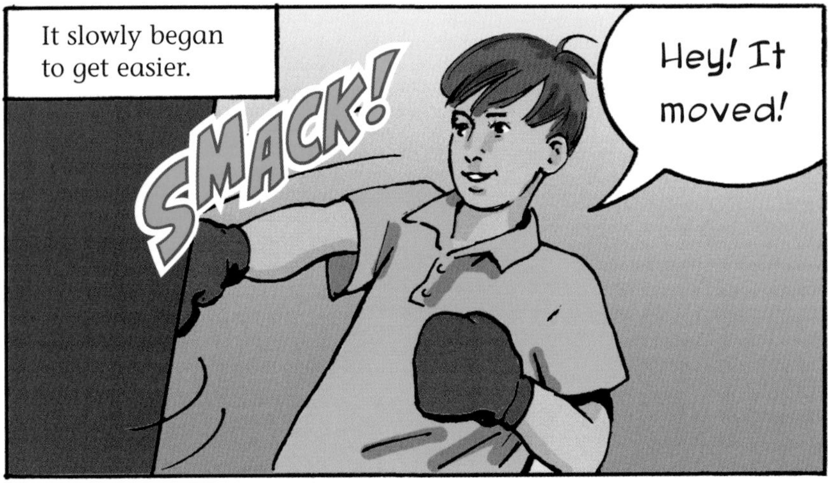
It slowly began to get easier.
SMACK!
Hey! It moved!

All the same, Scott soon felt he'd never done anything so tiring in his life. He was glad when it was Ali's turn. Of course, his friend had done this before, and Scott was impressed by the speed of his punches.

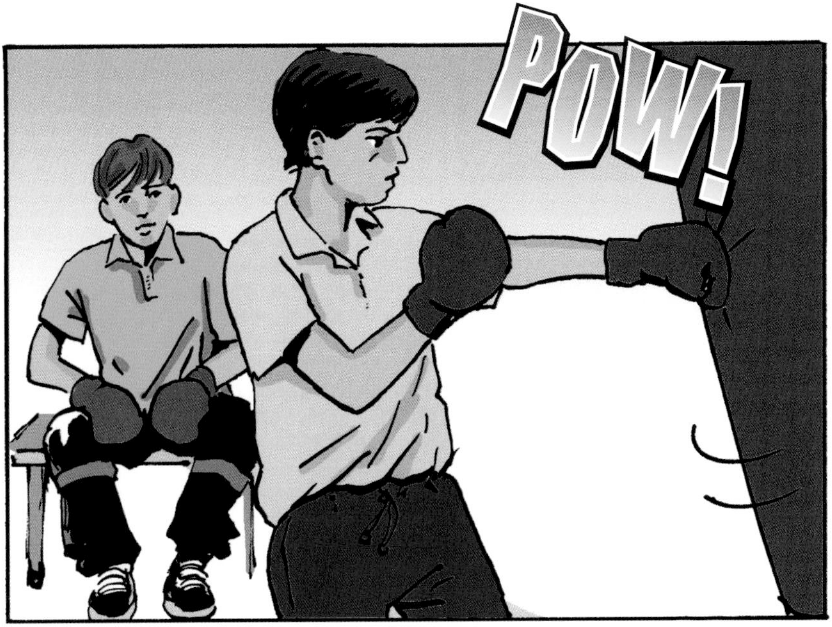
POW!

Ali could also manage to hit the same area. Scott's punches had landed all over the place.

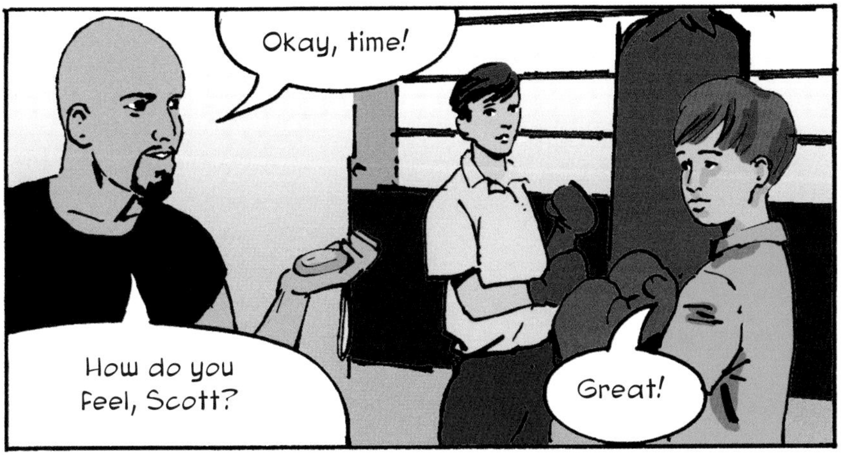
Okay, time!
How do you feel, Scott?
Great!

Scott had found his second round of punching just as tough as the first, but he wasn't going to admit it.

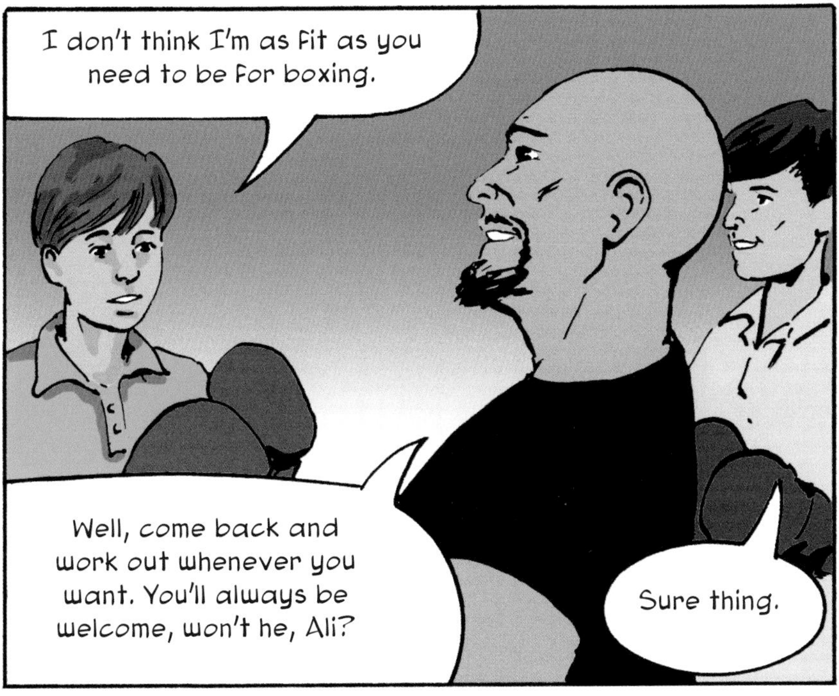
I don't think I'm as fit as you need to be for boxing.
Well, come back and work out whenever you want. You'll always be welcome, won't he, Ali?
Sure thing.

Then a few minutes later, they were all speeding back home in Mr. Hosein's sports car. Scott was aching in muscles he never knew he had, but he still felt he achieved something at the health club.

CHAPTER THREE

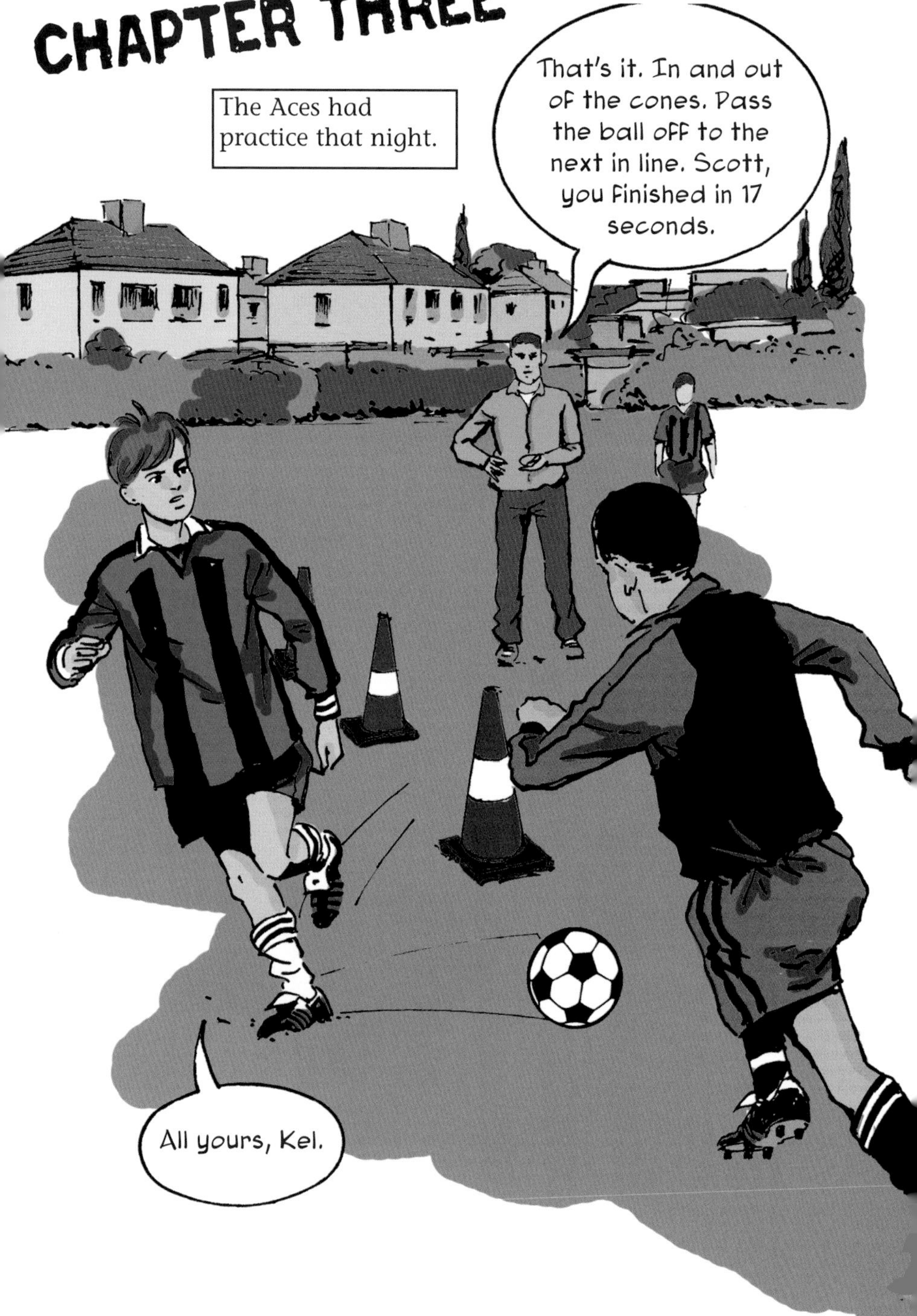
The Aces had practice that night.
That's it. In and out of the cones. Pass the ball off to the next in line. Scott, you finished in 17 seconds.
All yours, Kel.

After Kel had finished in a slightly faster time, he came over to Scott.

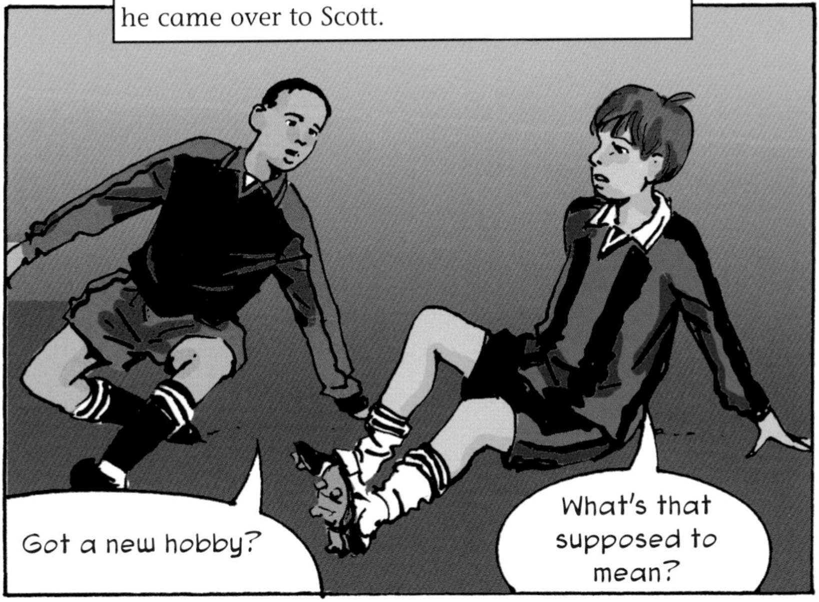
Got a new hobby?
What's that supposed to mean?

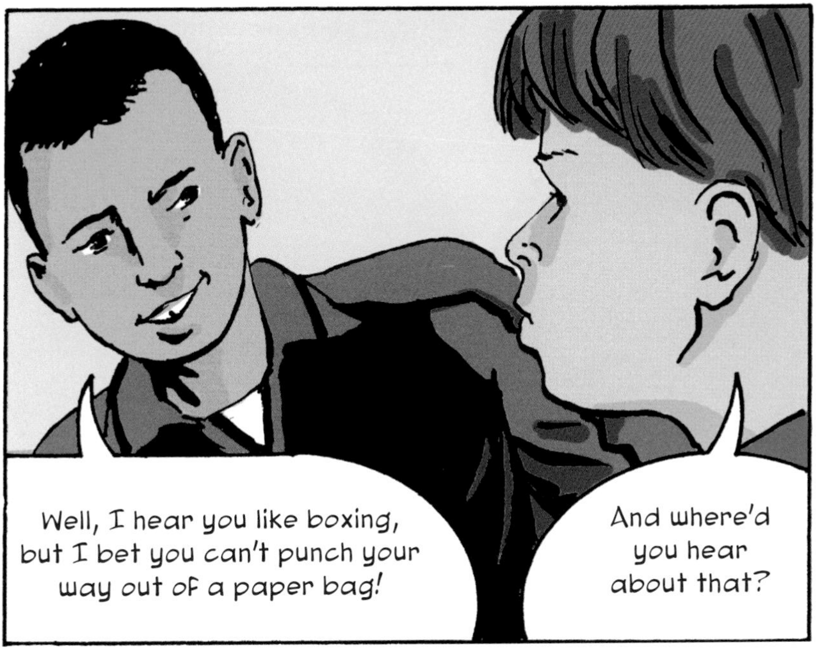
Well, I hear you like boxing, but I bet you can't punch your way out of a paper bag!
And where'd you hear about that?

Scott knew Ali hadn't been talking to Kel. They didn't even know each other. So how did Kel find out?

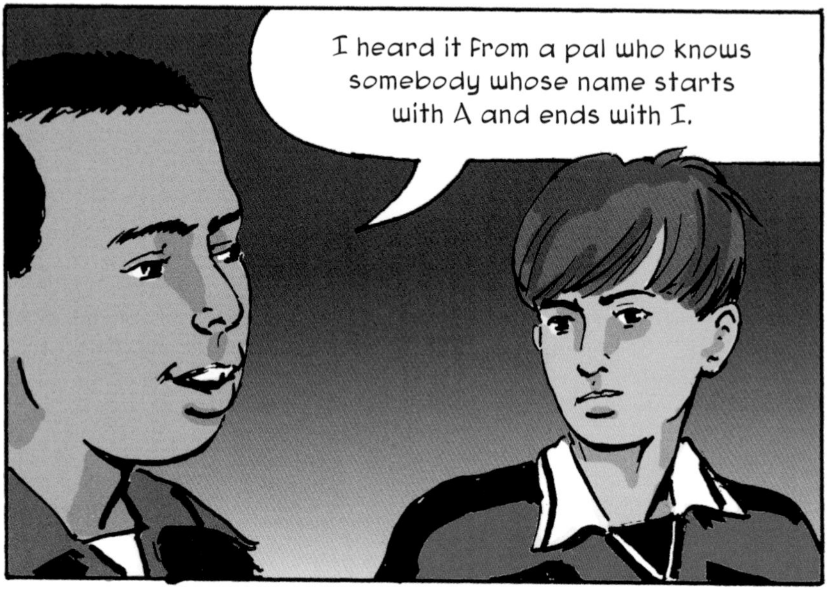
I heard it from a pal who knows somebody whose name starts with A and ends with I.

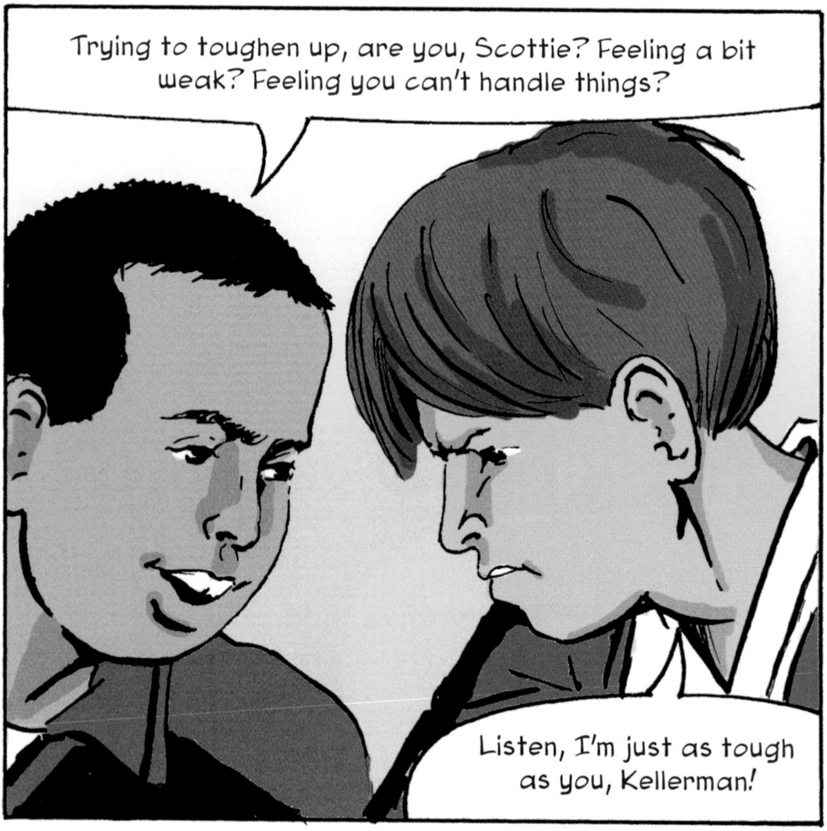
Trying to toughen up, are you, Scottie? Feeling a bit weak? Feeling you can't handle things?
Listen, I'm just as tough as you, Kellerman!

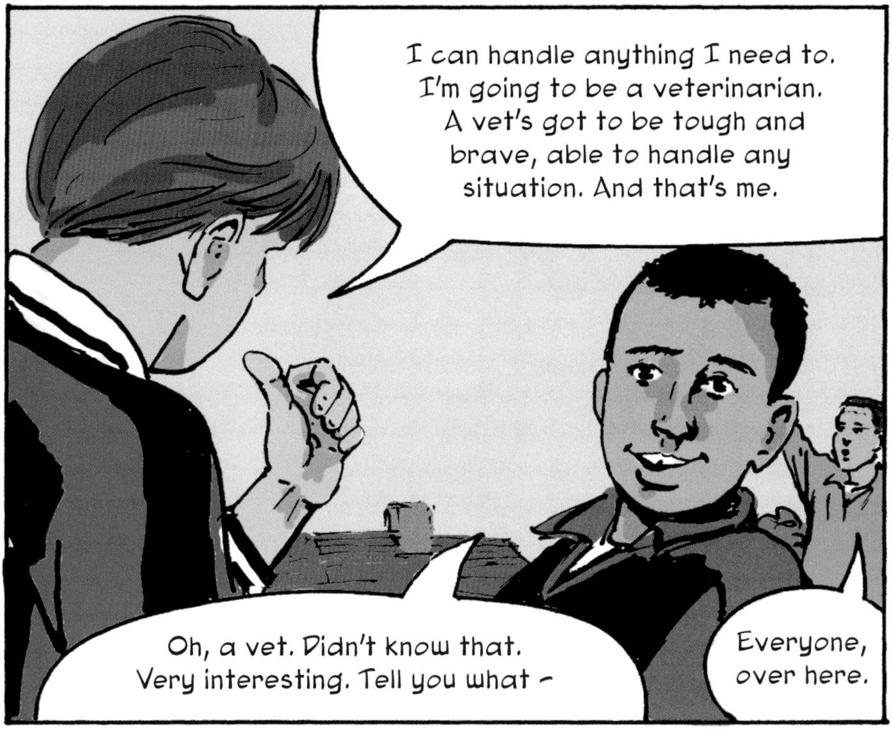
I can handle anything I need to. I'm going to be a veterinarian. A vet's got to be tough and brave, able to handle any situation. And that's me.
Oh, a vet. Didn't know that. Very interesting. Tell you what –
Everyone, over here.

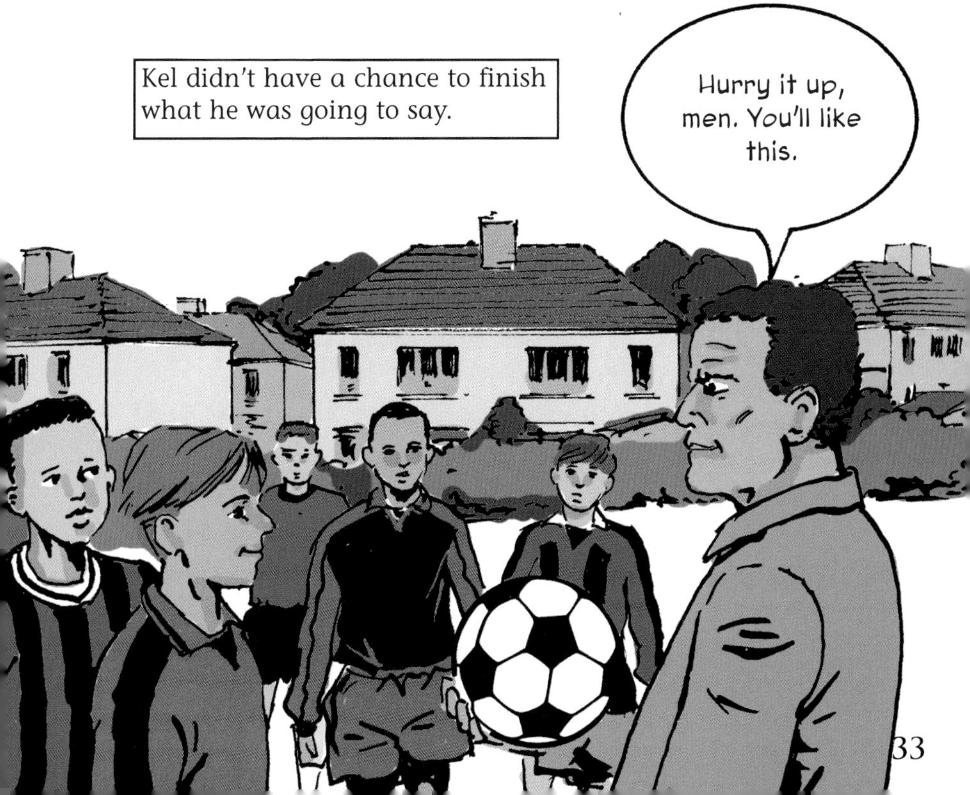
Kel didn't have a chance to finish what he was going to say.
Hurry it up, men. You'll like this.

It turned out to be a game of head tennis. Although Scott was one of the shorter players, he had good spring in his legs and could jump higher than many of the others.

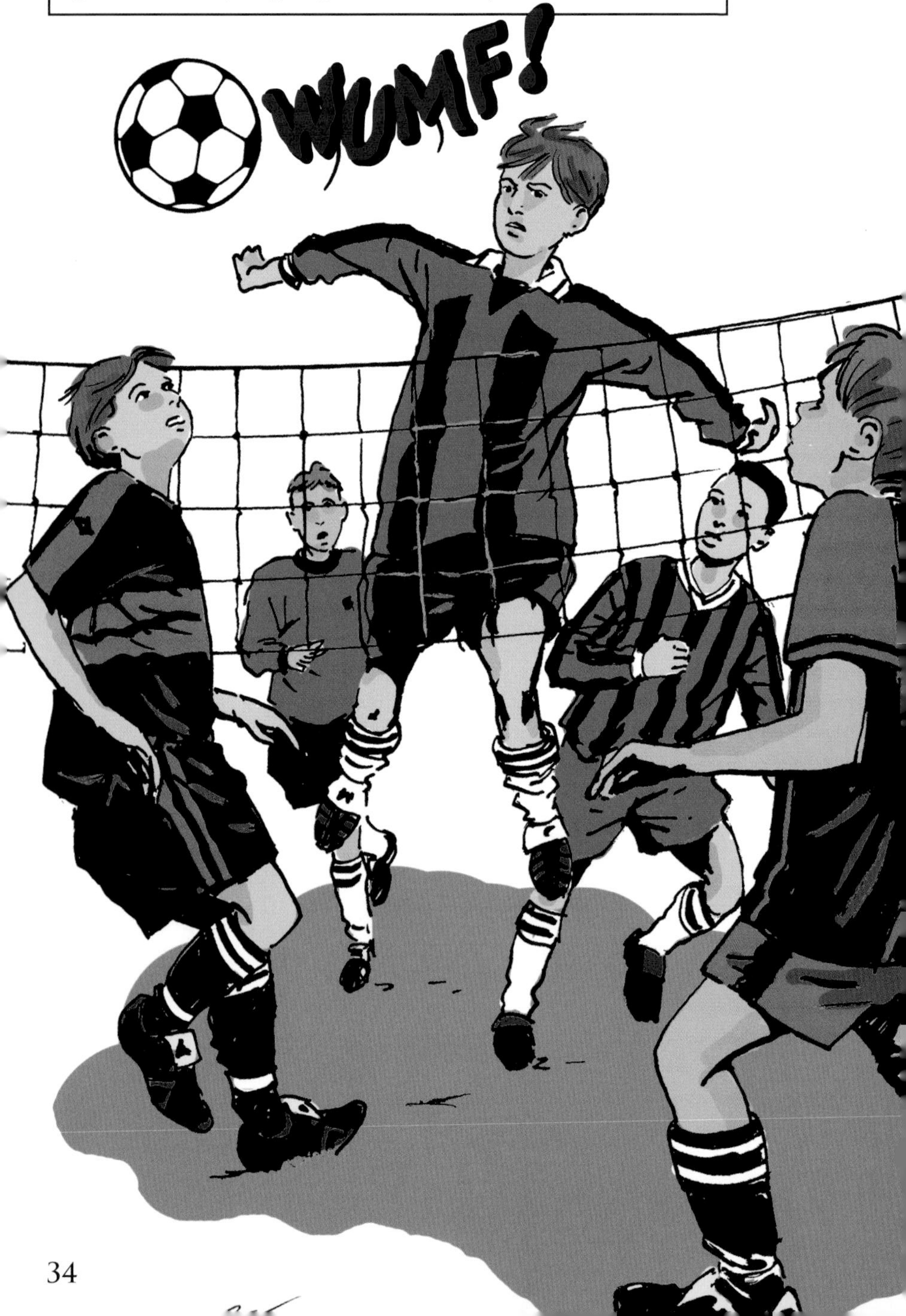
WUMF!

In spite of his height advantage, Kel wasn't very accurate with his headers.

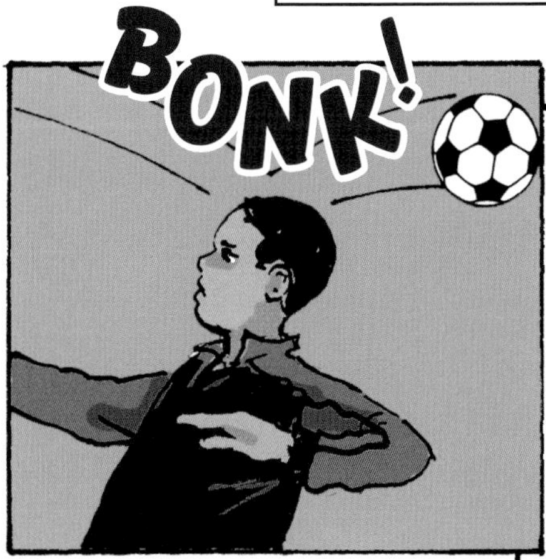
BONK!

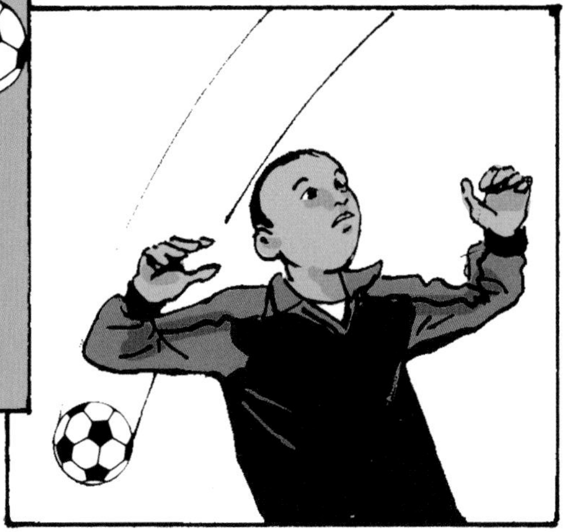

On one occasion, he missed the ball completely.

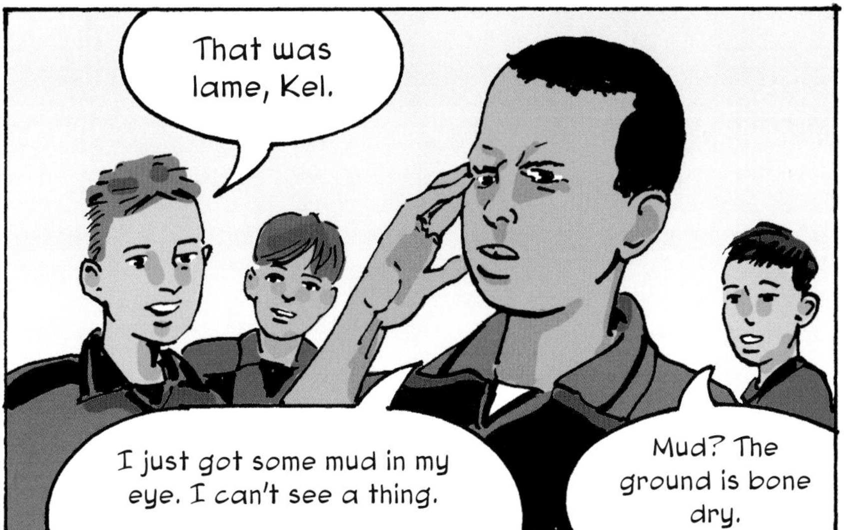
That was lame, Kel.
I just got some mud in my eye. I can't see a thing.
Mud? The ground is bone dry.

They didn't have a practice game, and Scott wasn't able to show Coach Royce how fast he could react to things on the field. Scott was worried that the coach would drop him before he had a chance to prove he could score whenever he was in sight of a goal.

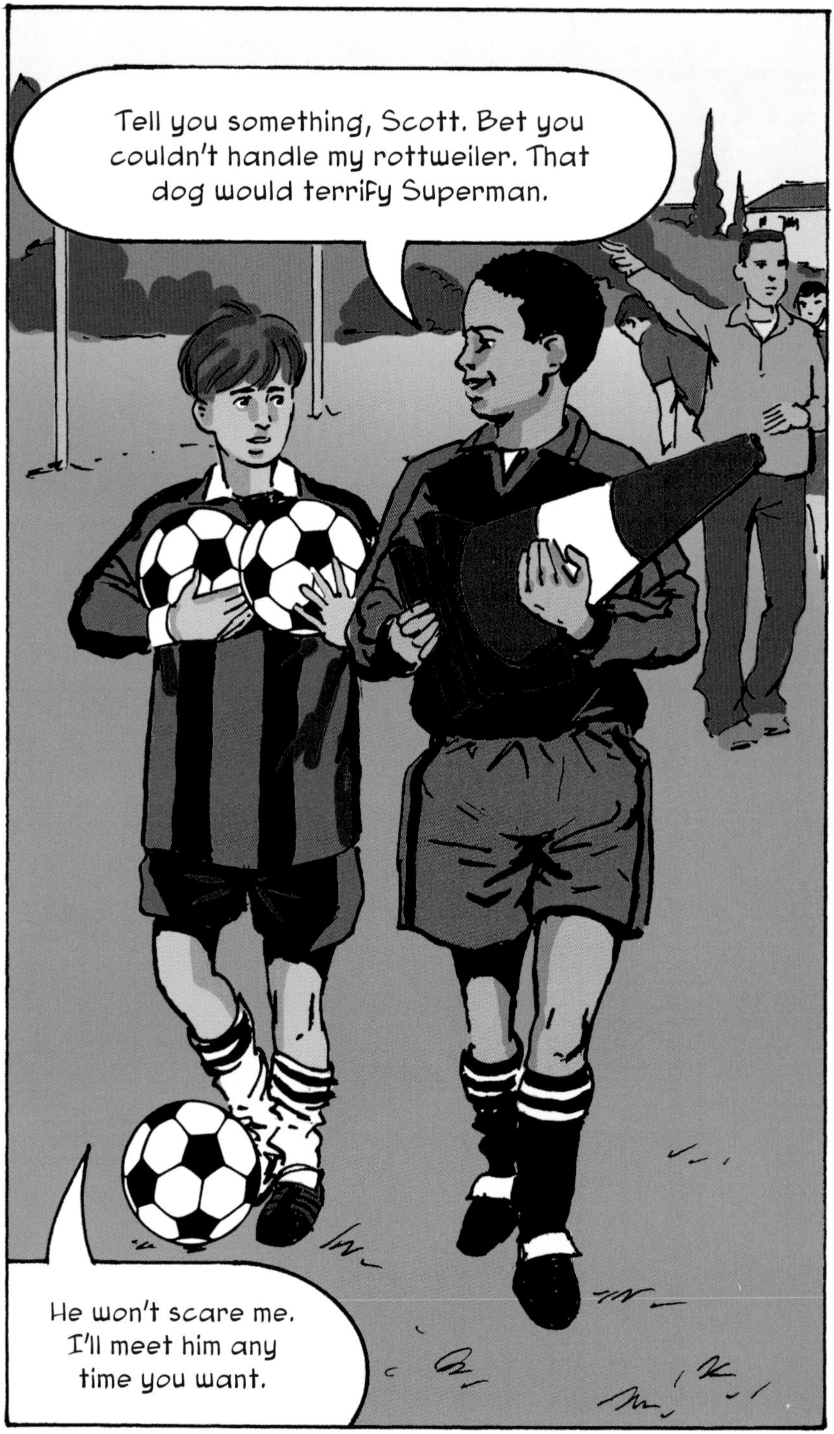
Tell you something, Scott. Bet you couldn't handle my rottweiler. That dog would terrify Superman.
He won't scare me. I'll meet him any time you want.

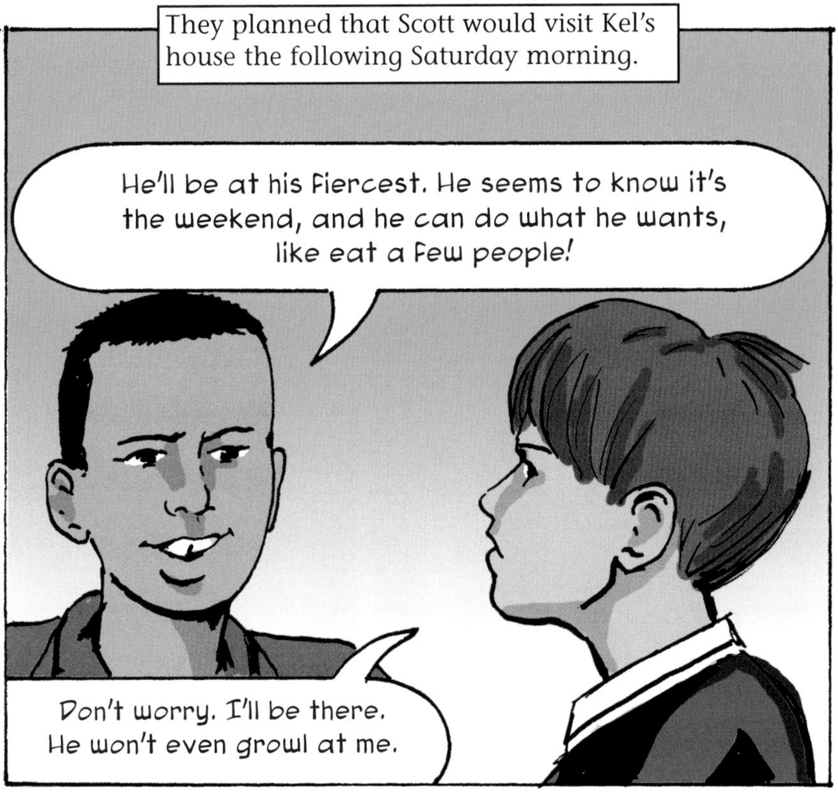
They planned that Scott would visit Kel's house the following Saturday morning.
He'll be at his fiercest. He seems to know it's the weekend, and he can do what he wants, like eat a few people!
Don't worry. I'll be there. He won't even growl at me.

Scott always got along well with animals and never felt afraid of them. Somehow they seemed to sense he cared for them.

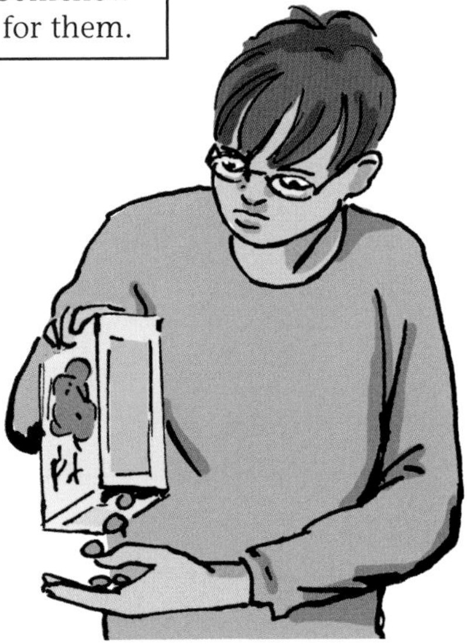

As a small boy, he decided he wanted to be a vet. After all, he could still play soccer in his spare time. However, he knew how aggressive a rottweiler could be. So he took some pet treats with him just in case.

CHAPTER FOUR

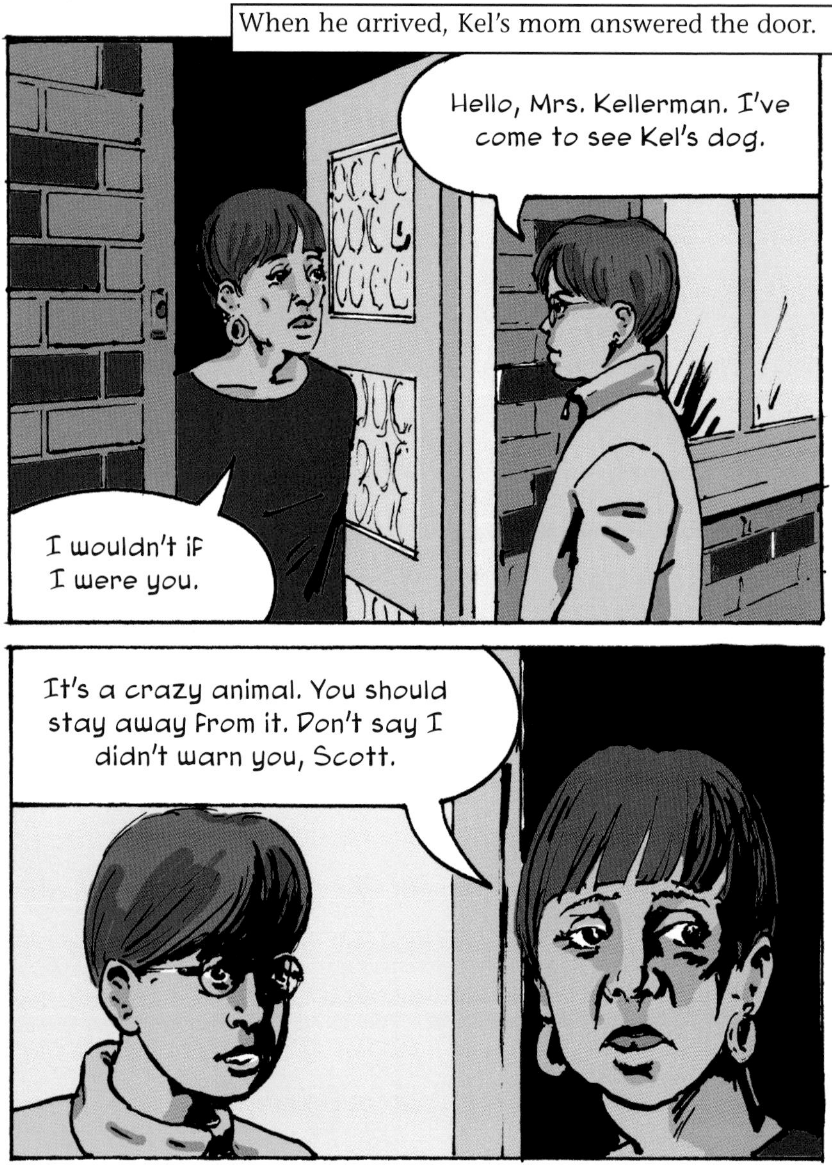
When he arrived, Kel's mom answered the door.
Hello, Mrs. Kellerman. I've come to see Kel's dog.
I wouldn't if I were you.
It's a crazy animal. You should stay away from it. Don't say I didn't warn you, Scott.

For the first time, Scott felt a little nervous. If Kel's mom worried about the rottweiler, then it might be wilder than he imagined.

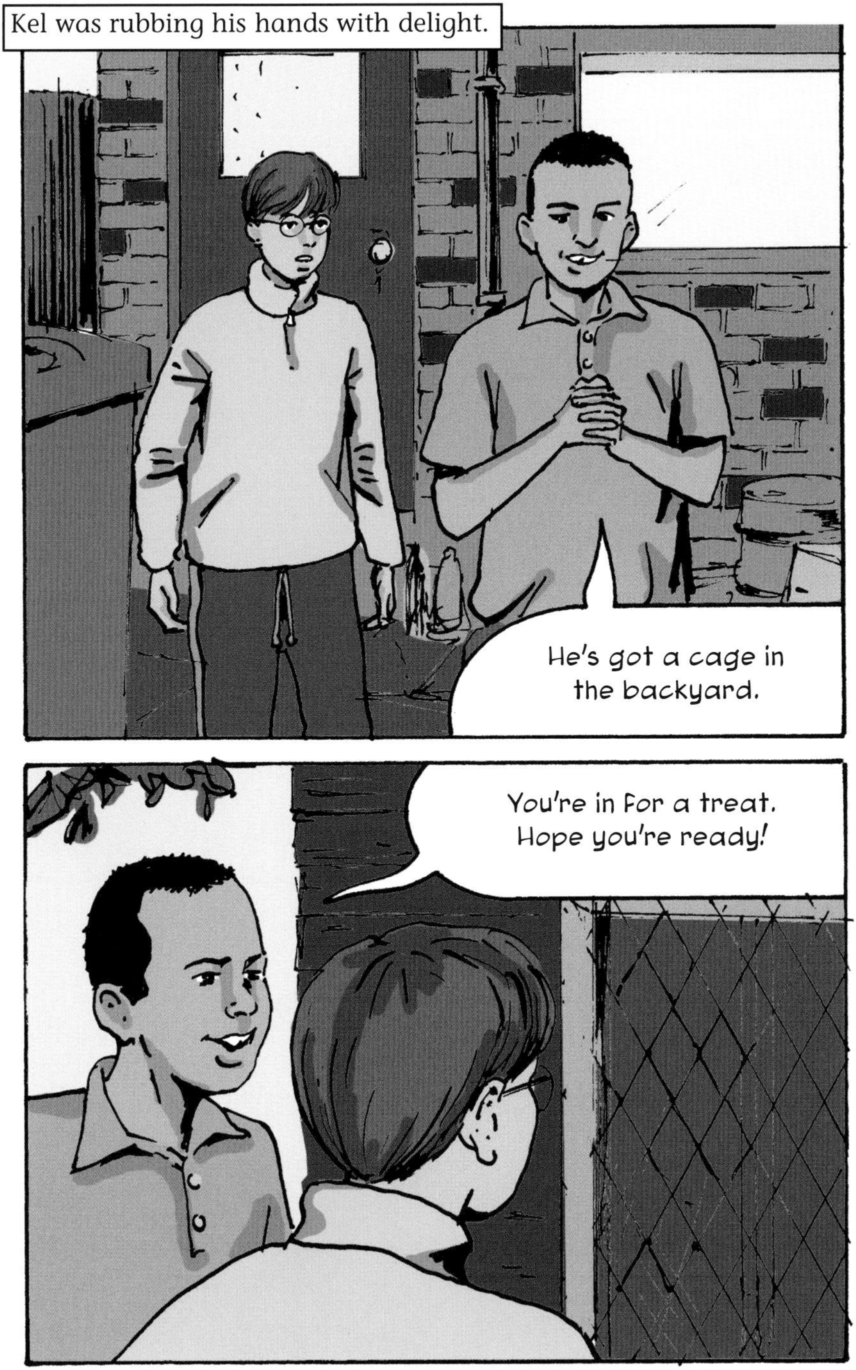
Kel was rubbing his hands with delight.
He's got a cage in the backyard.
You're in for a treat. Hope you're ready!

Frenzied barking started the moment the animal sensed a stranger was present. Kel was already talking to the dog as they approached the cage, but that made no difference.

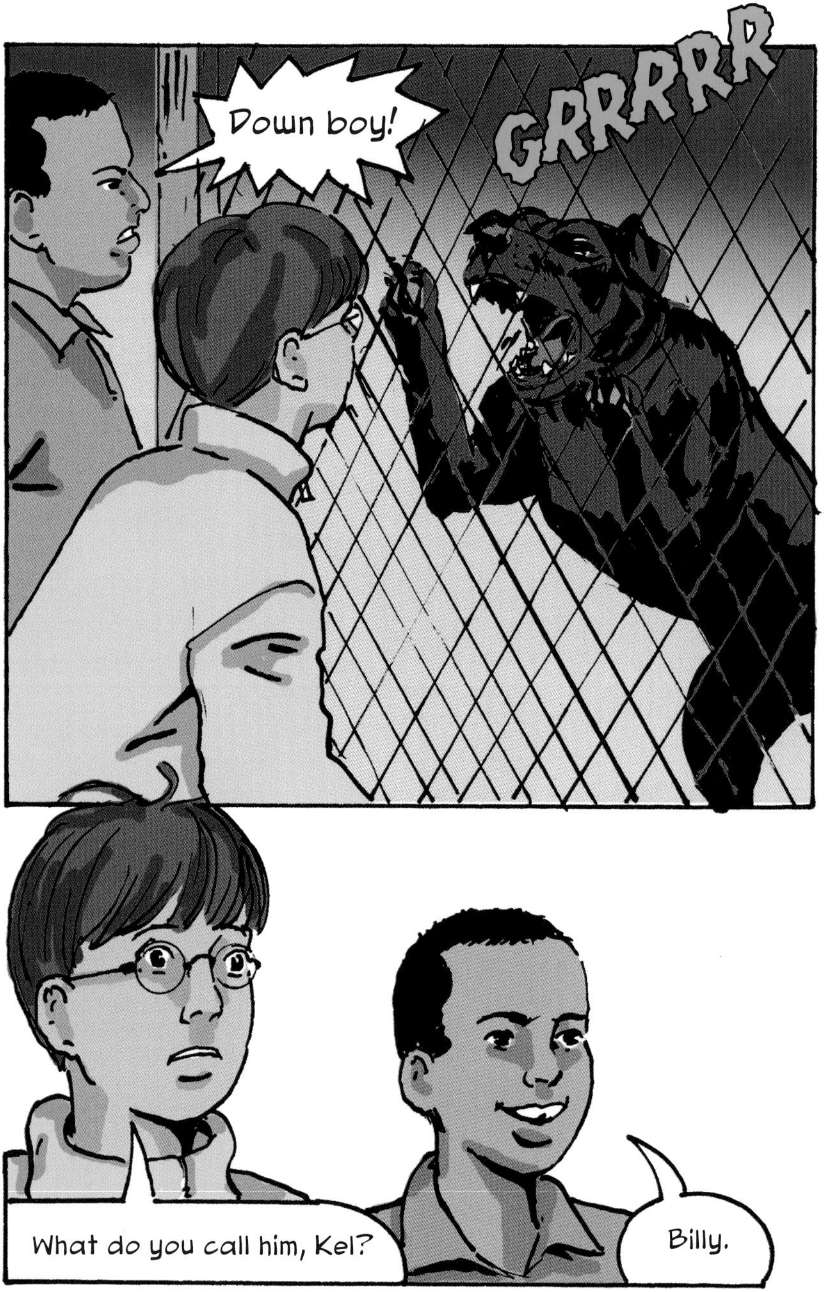

Down boy!
GRRRRR
What do you call him, Kel?
Billy.

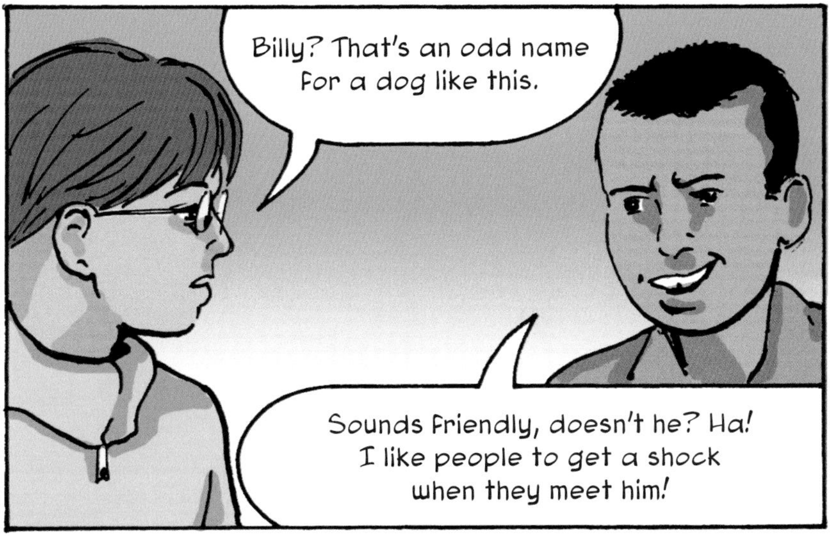
Billy? That's an odd name for a dog like this.
Sounds friendly, doesn't he? Ha! I like people to get a shock when they meet him!

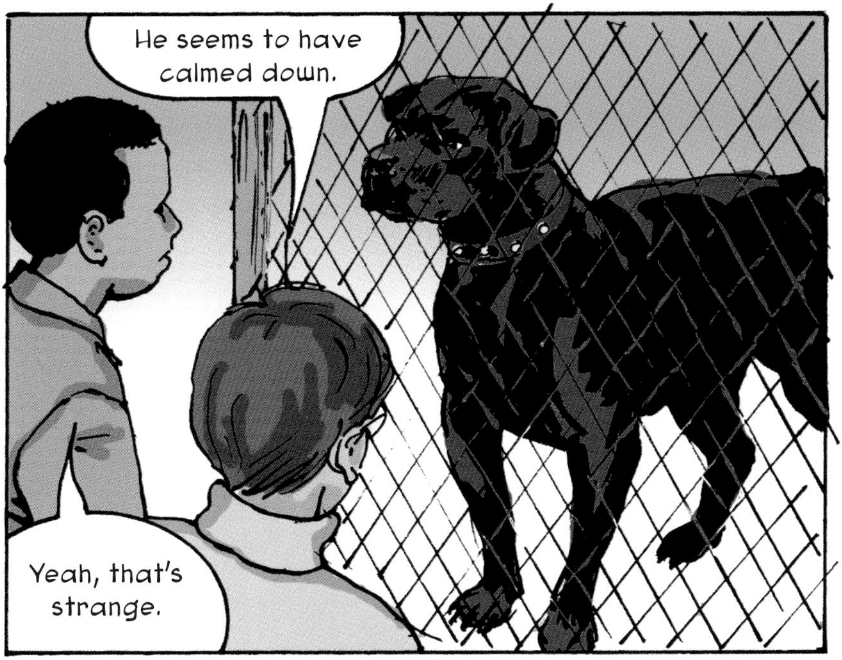
He seems to have calmed down.
Yeah, that's strange.

Billy's frantic barking stopped completely. There weren't any growls, and the hair on his coat was flat. All his aggression seemed to have vanished. He looked as if he were listening to their conversation.

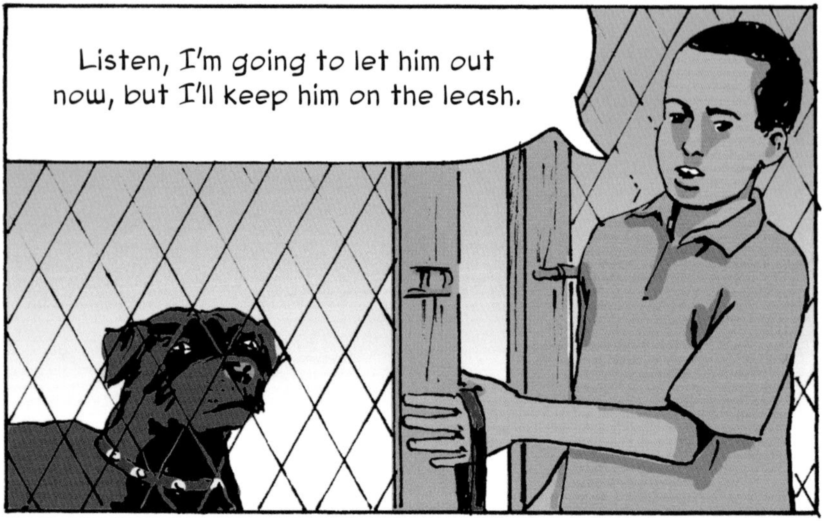
Listen, I'm going to let him out now, but I'll keep him on the leash.

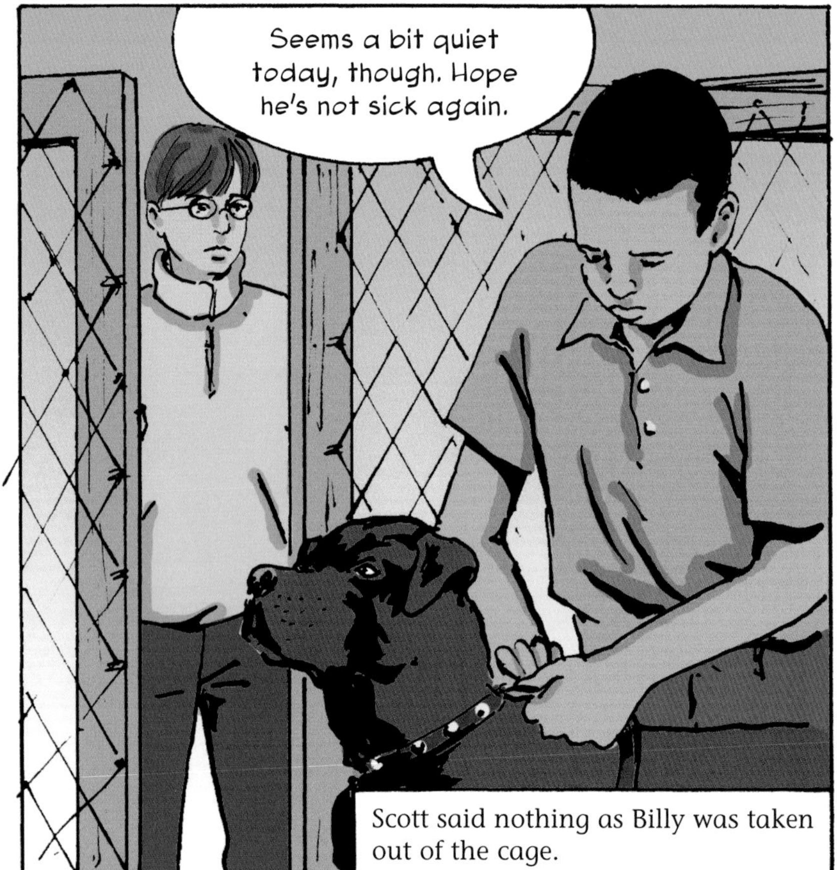
Seems a bit quiet today, though. Hope he's not sick again.
Scott said nothing as Billy was taken out of the cage.

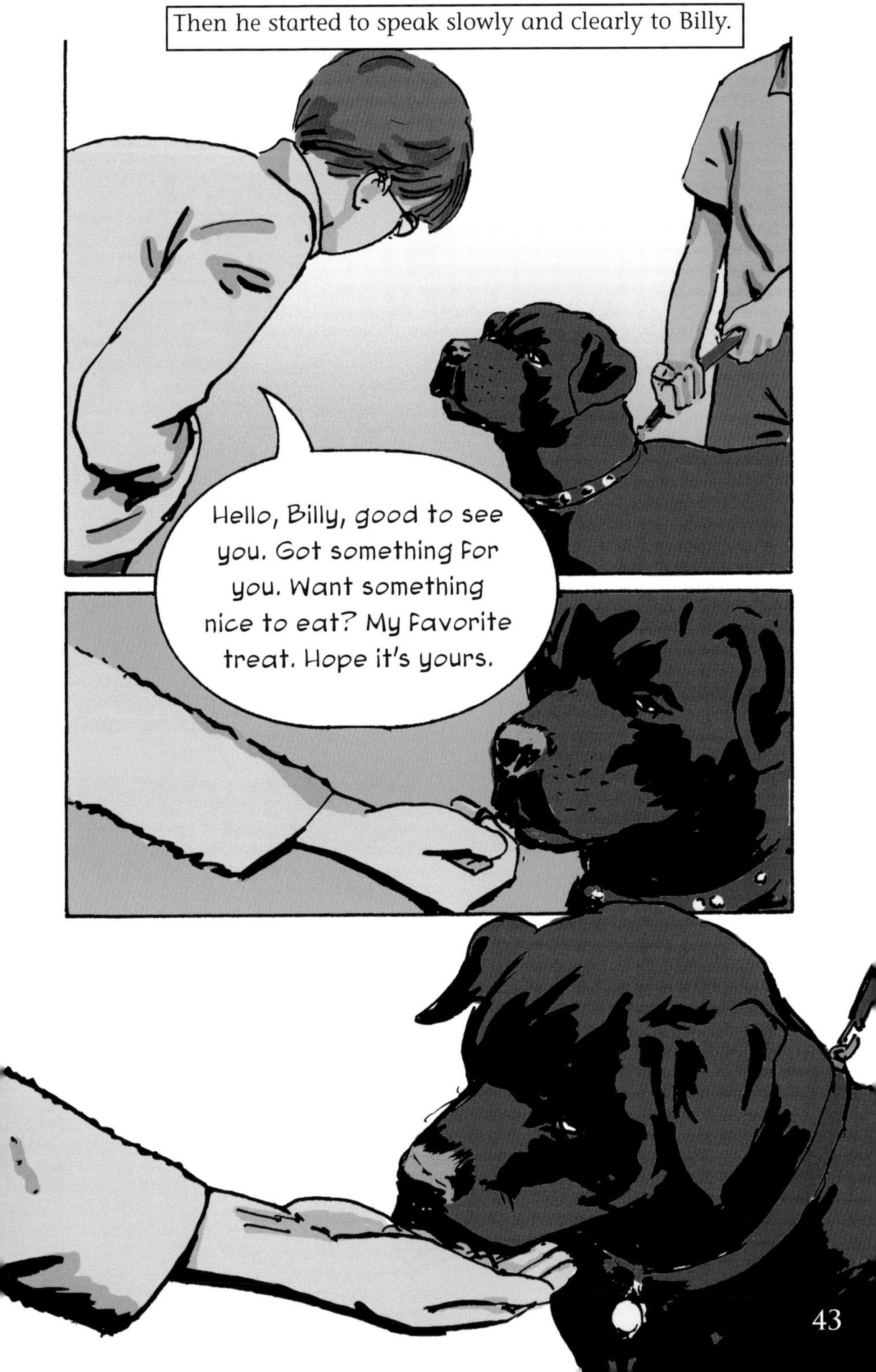
Then he started to speak slowly and clearly to Billy.
Hello, Billy, good to see you. Got something for you. Want something nice to eat? My favorite treat. Hope it's yours.

Kel kept blinking as if he couldn't believe what was happening.

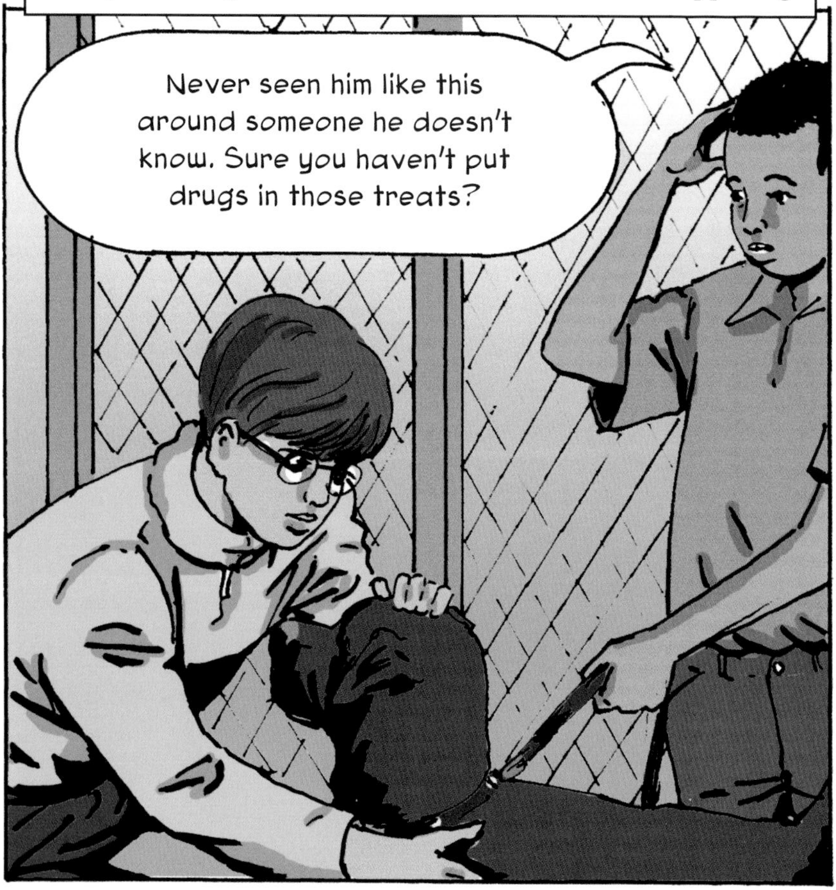

Never seen him like this around someone he doesn't know. Sure you haven't put drugs in those treats?

Scott was concerned about Billy.

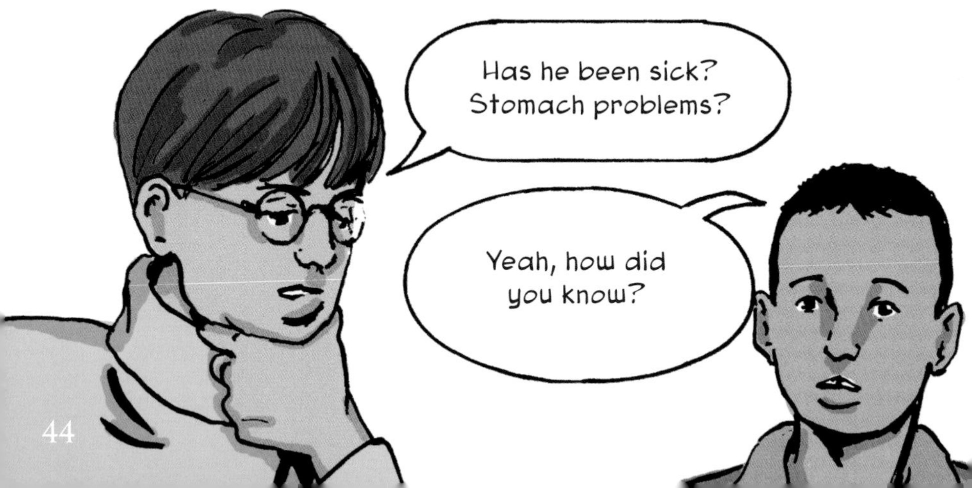

Has he been sick? Stomach problems?
Yeah, how did you know?

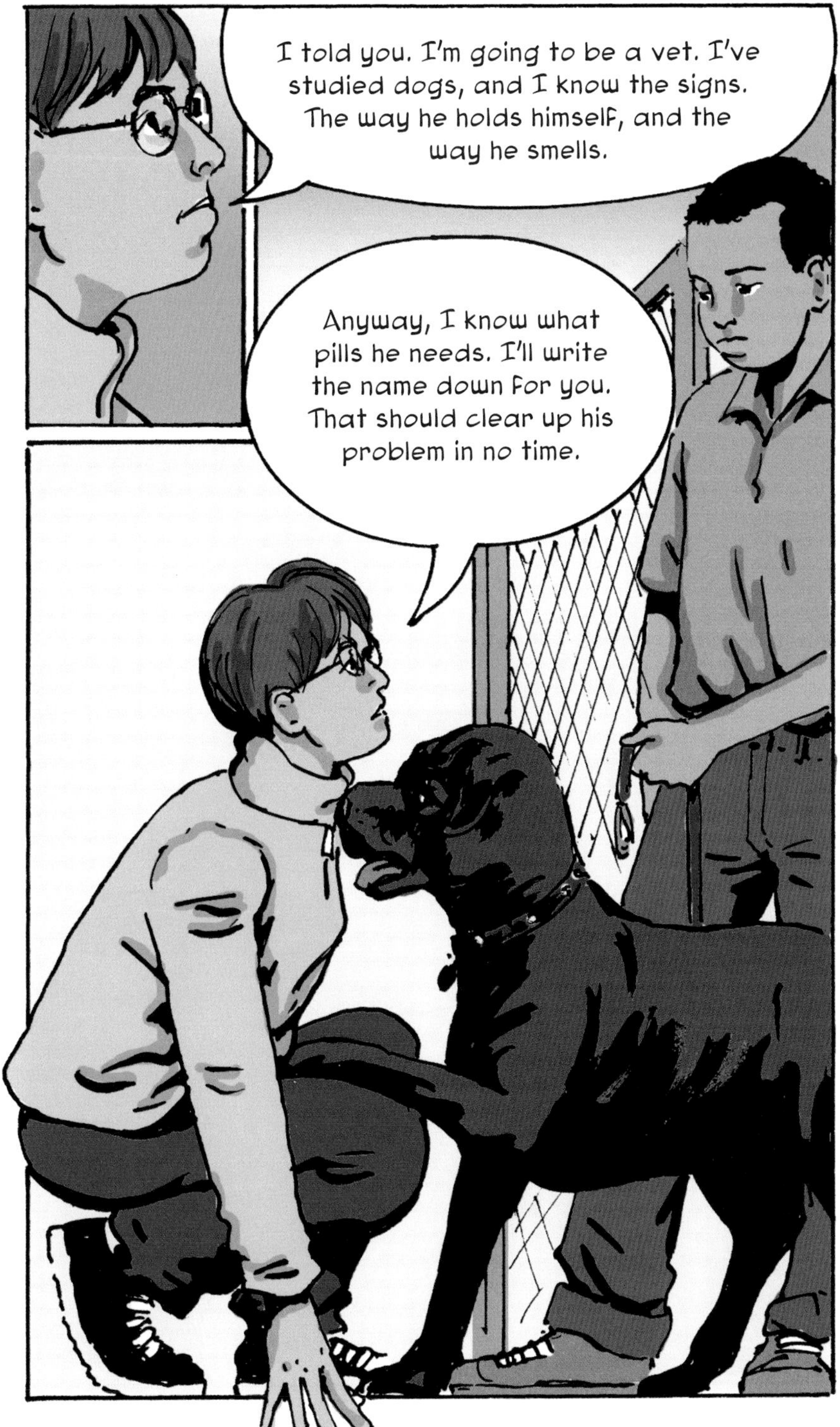
I told you. I'm going to be a vet. I've studied dogs, and I know the signs. The way he holds himself, and the way he smells.
Anyway, I know what pills he needs. I'll write the name down for you. That should clear up his problem in no time.

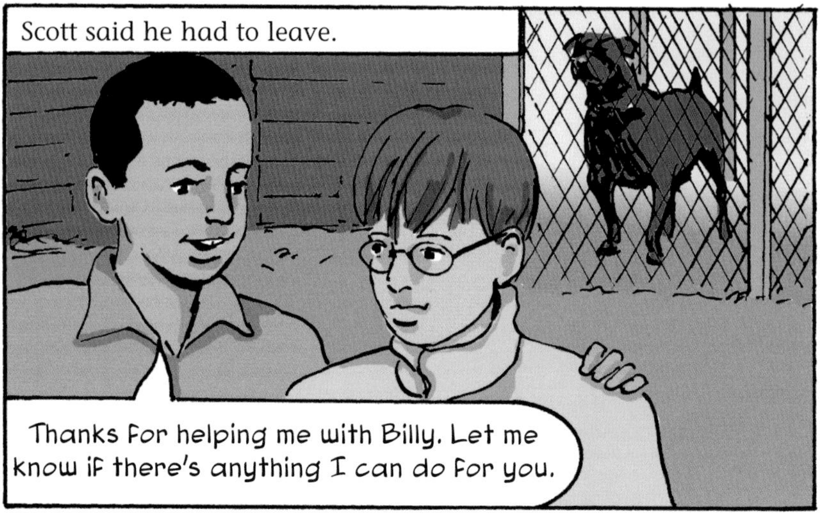
Scott said he had to leave.
Thanks for helping me with Billy. Let me know if there's anything I can do for you.

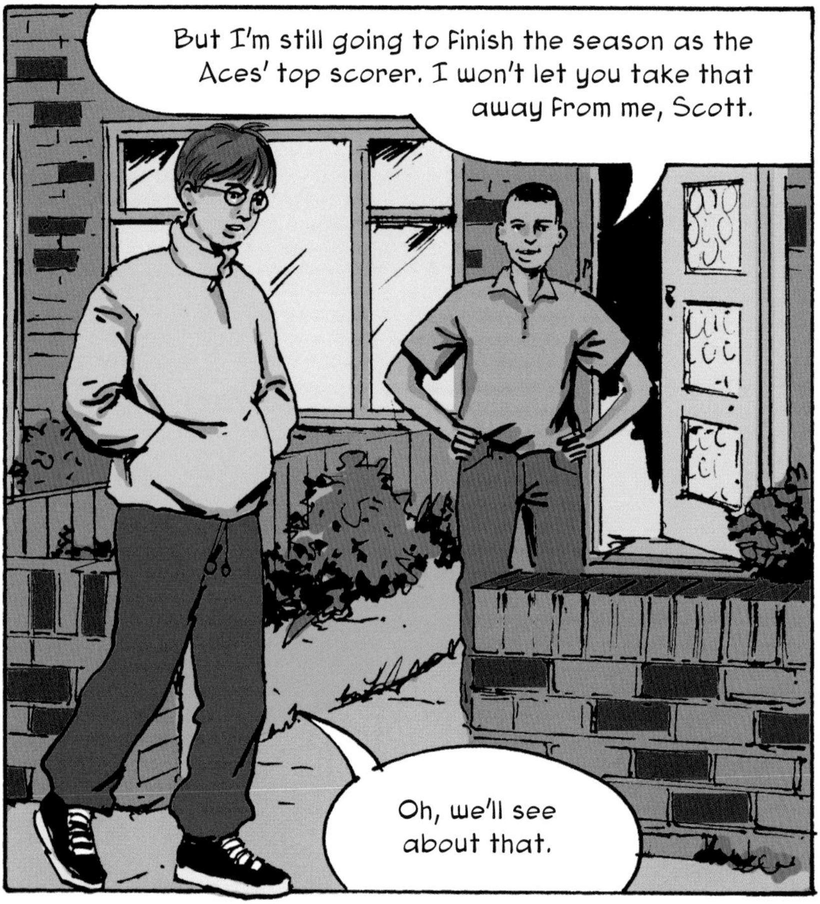
But I'm still going to finish the season as the Aces' top scorer. I won't let you take that away from me, Scott.
Oh, we'll see about that.

CHAPTER FIVE

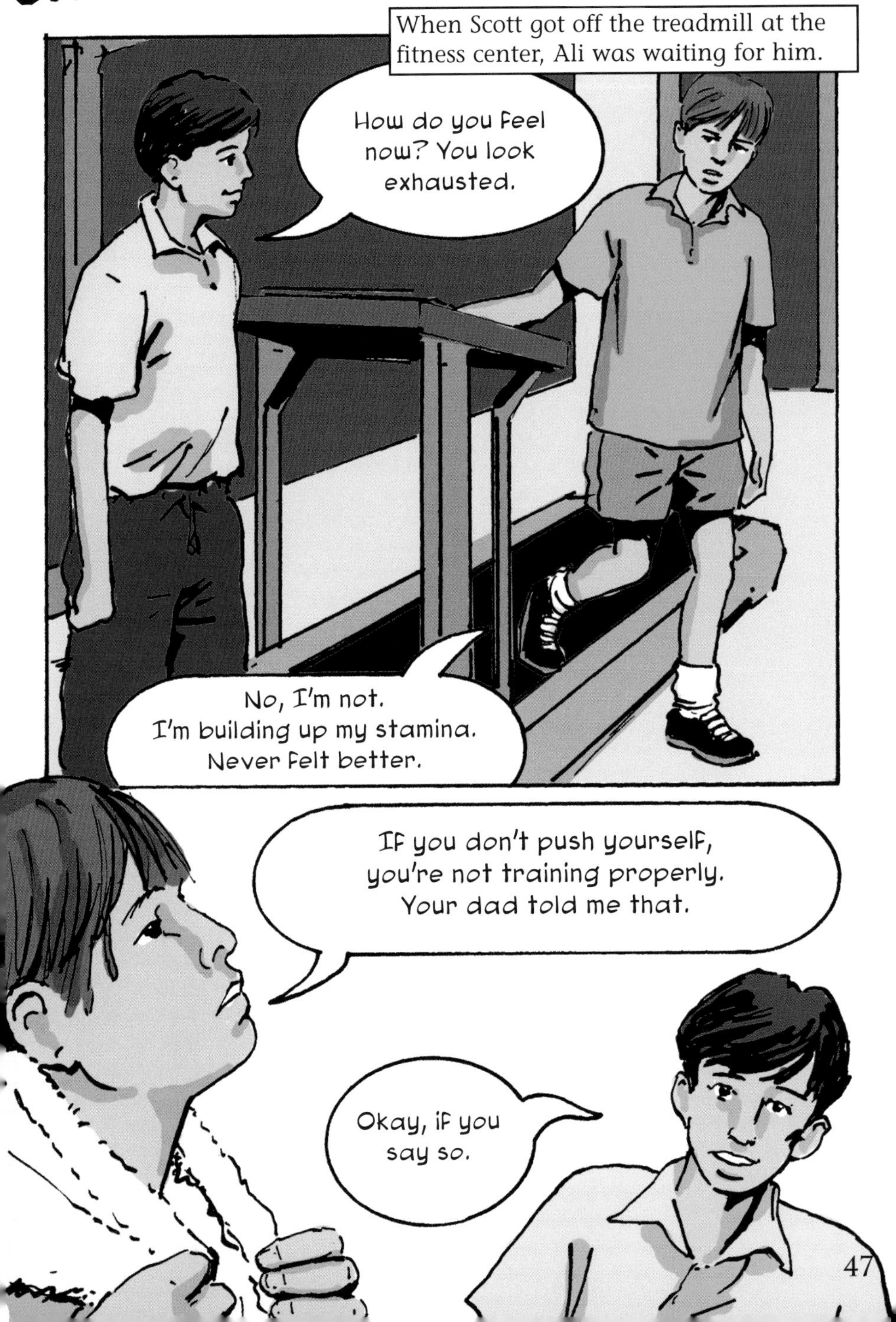
When Scott got off the treadmill at the fitness center, Ali was waiting for him.
How do you feel now? You look exhausted.
No, I'm not. I'm building up my stamina. Never felt better.
If you don't push yourself, you're not training properly. Your dad told me that.
Okay, if you say so.

Scott wanted to be in top form for the Aces' away game at Weather Hill, one of the league's worst teams. Scott saw it as a chance to increase his goal total and catch up to Kel. Kel was worried because he hurt his ankle during practice. Coach Royce had lined up a replacement, Warren, in case Kel couldn't play. Warren had never played a full game for them so far and had only been a sub a couple of times.

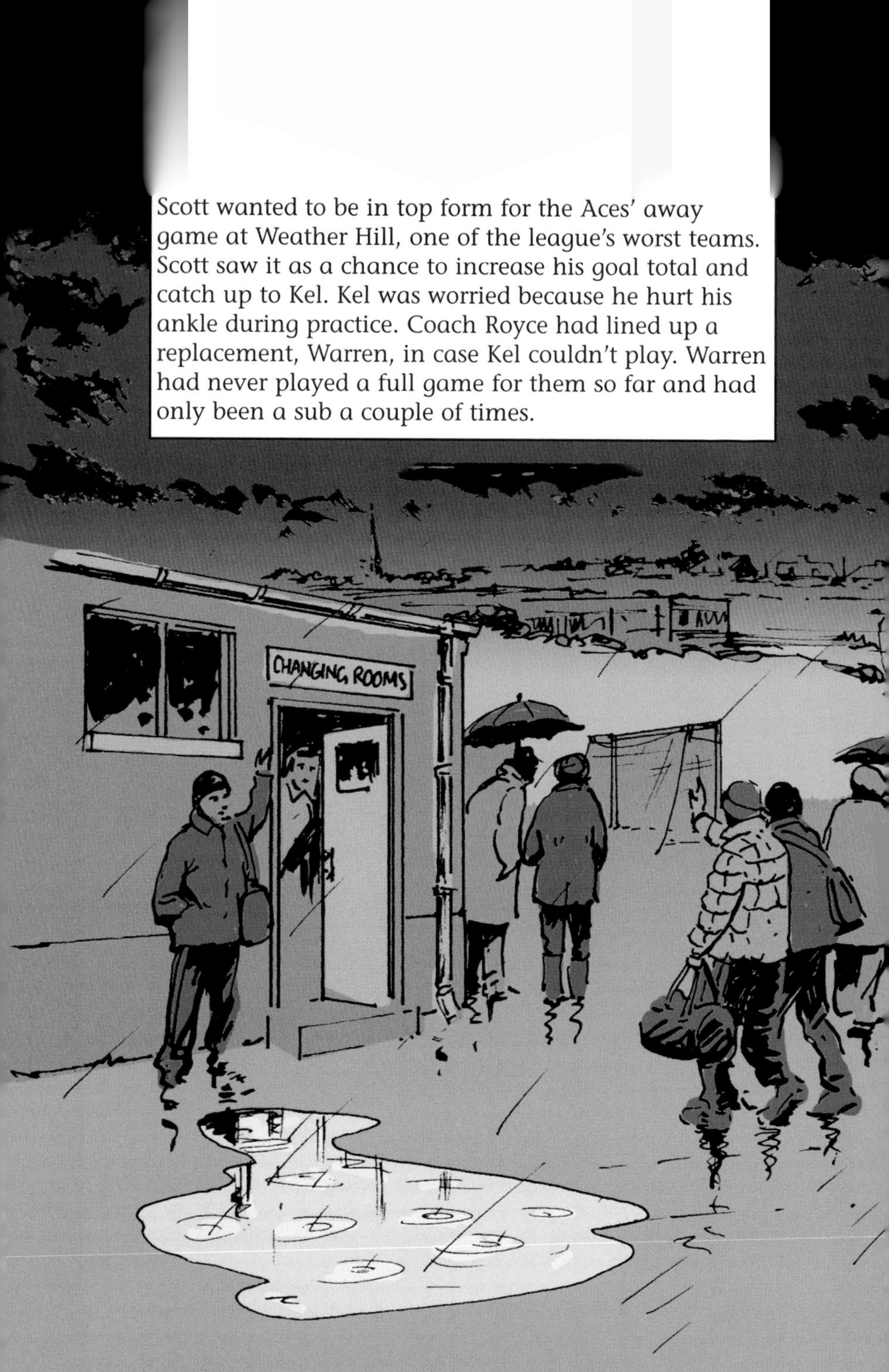
CHANGING ROOMS

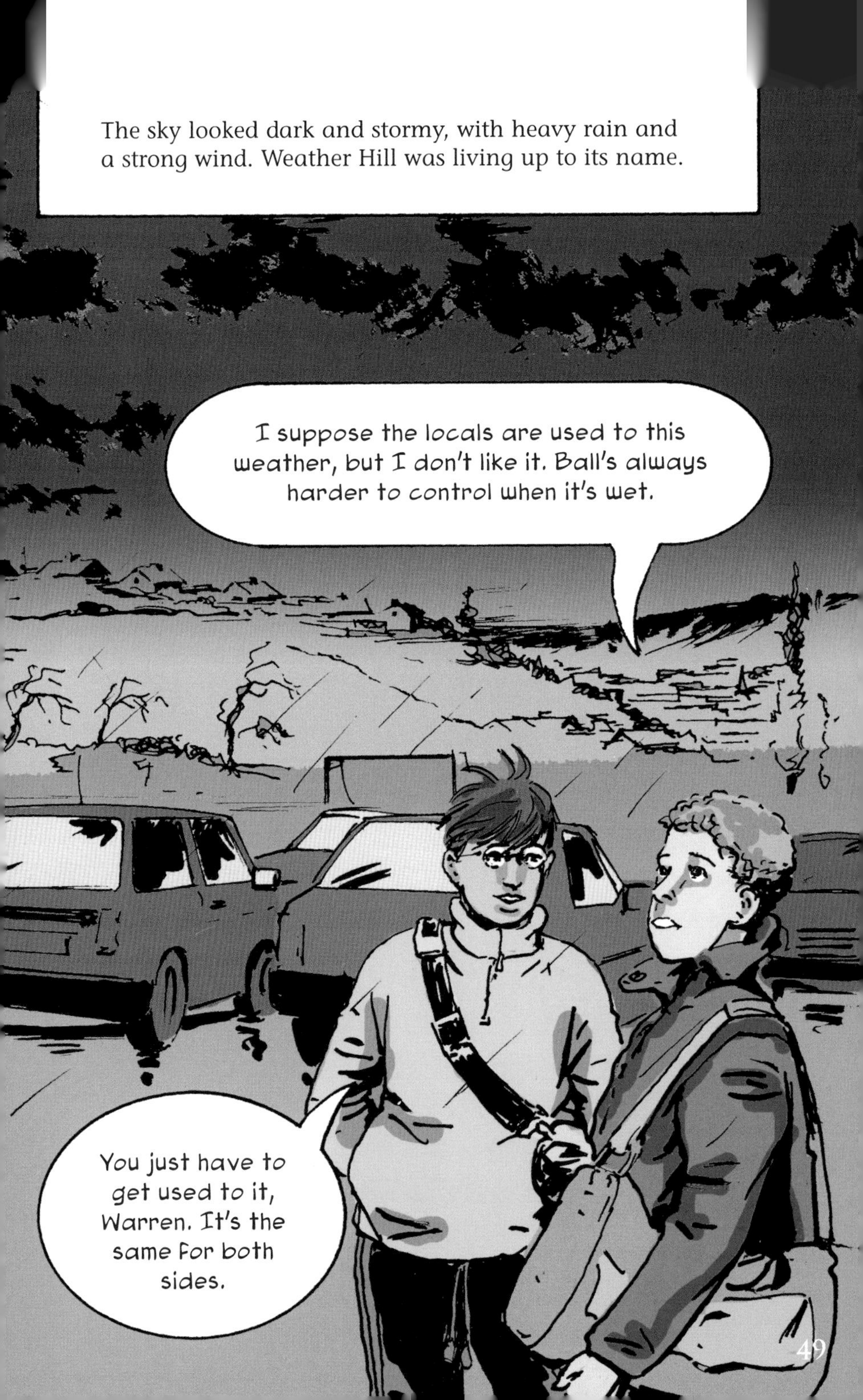
The sky looked dark and stormy, with heavy rain and a strong wind. Weather Hill was living up to its name.
I suppose the locals are used to this weather, but I don't like it. Ball's always harder to control when it's wet.
You just have to get used to it, Warren. It's the same for both sides.

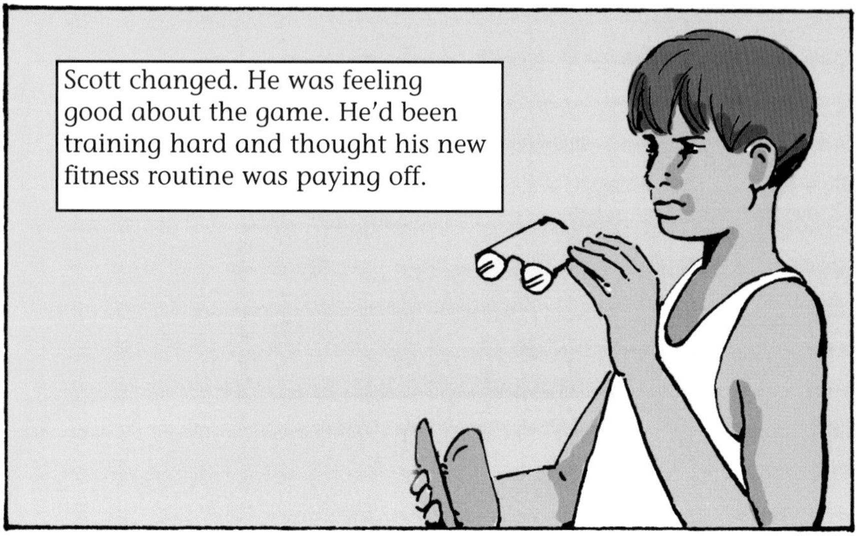
Scott changed. He was feeling good about the game. He'd been training hard and thought his new fitness routine was paying off.

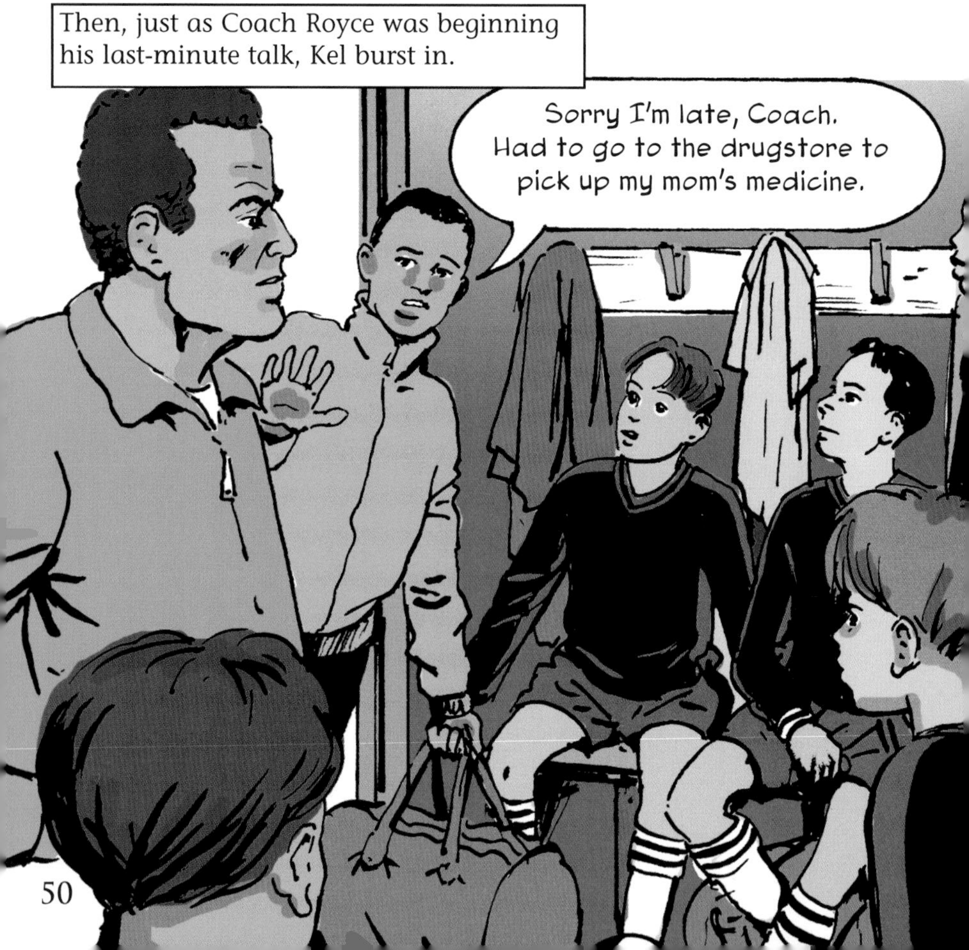
Then, just as Coach Royce was beginning his last-minute talk, Kel burst in.
Sorry I'm late, Coach. Had to go to the drugstore to pick up my mom's medicine.

With an explanation like that, the coach couldn't blame his leading scorer for his lateness.

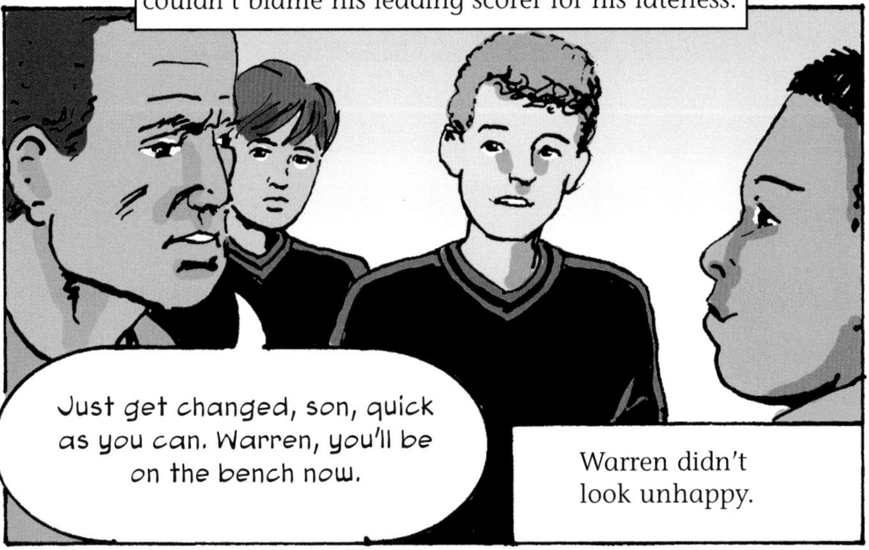
Just get changed, son, quick as you can. Warren, you'll be on the bench now.
Warren didn't look unhappy.

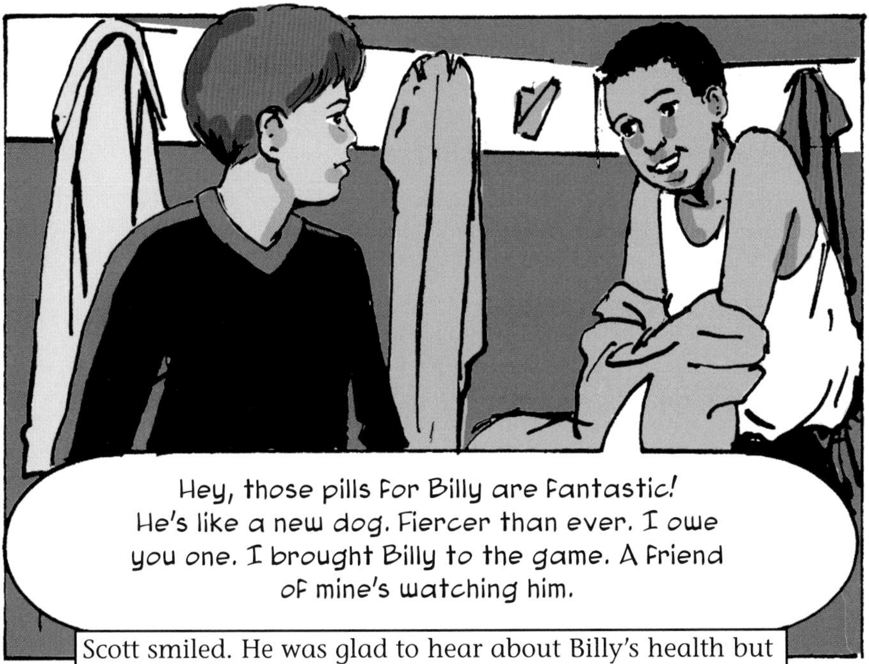
Hey, those pills for Billy are fantastic! He's like a new dog. Fiercer than ever. I owe you one. I brought Billy to the game. A friend of mine's watching him.

Scott smiled. He was glad to hear about Billy's health but disappointed that Kel would get the chance to add to his goal total after all. And Kel was in the best of moods.

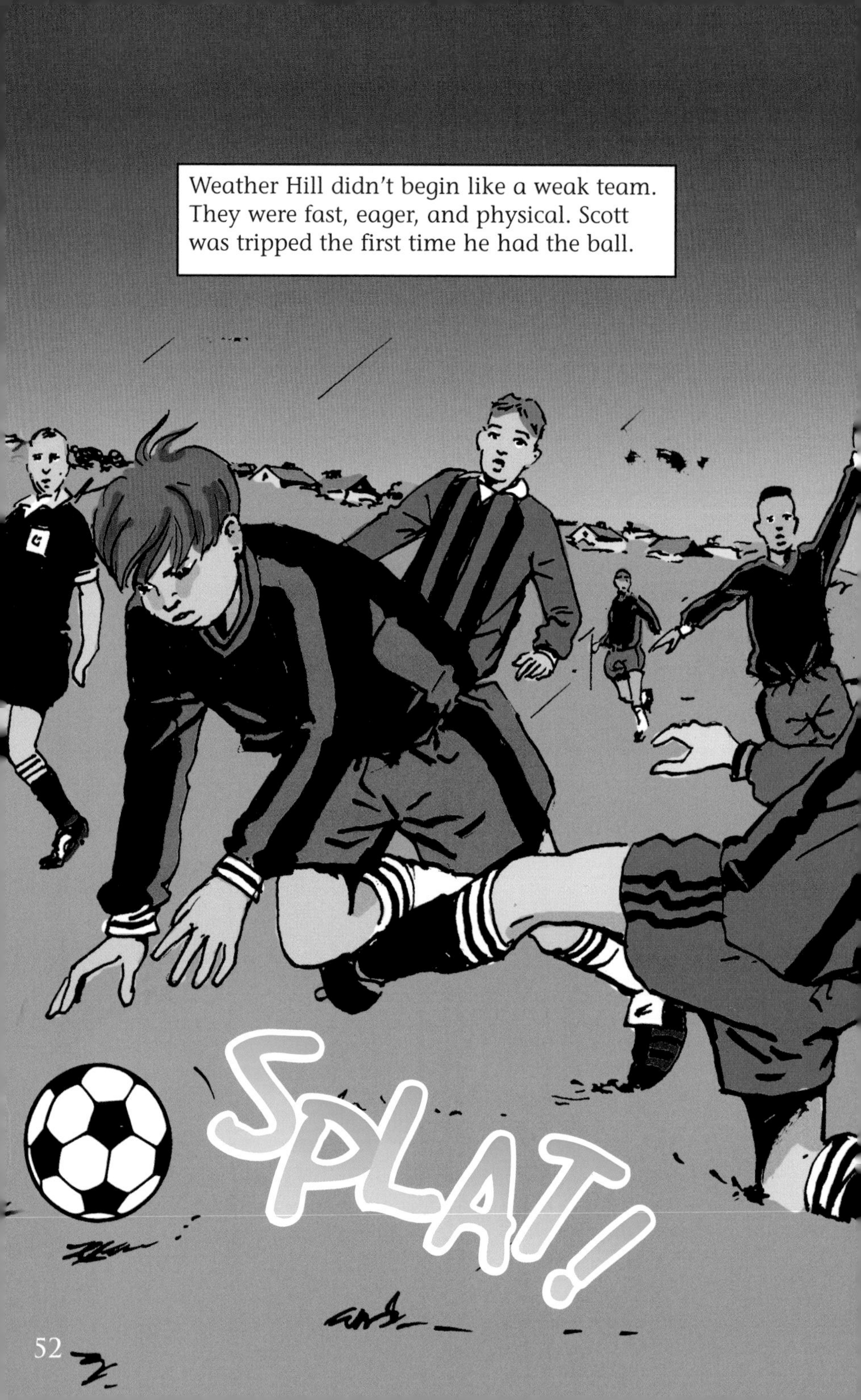
Weather Hill didn't begin like a weak team. They were fast, eager, and physical. Scott was tripped the first time he had the ball.
SPLAT!

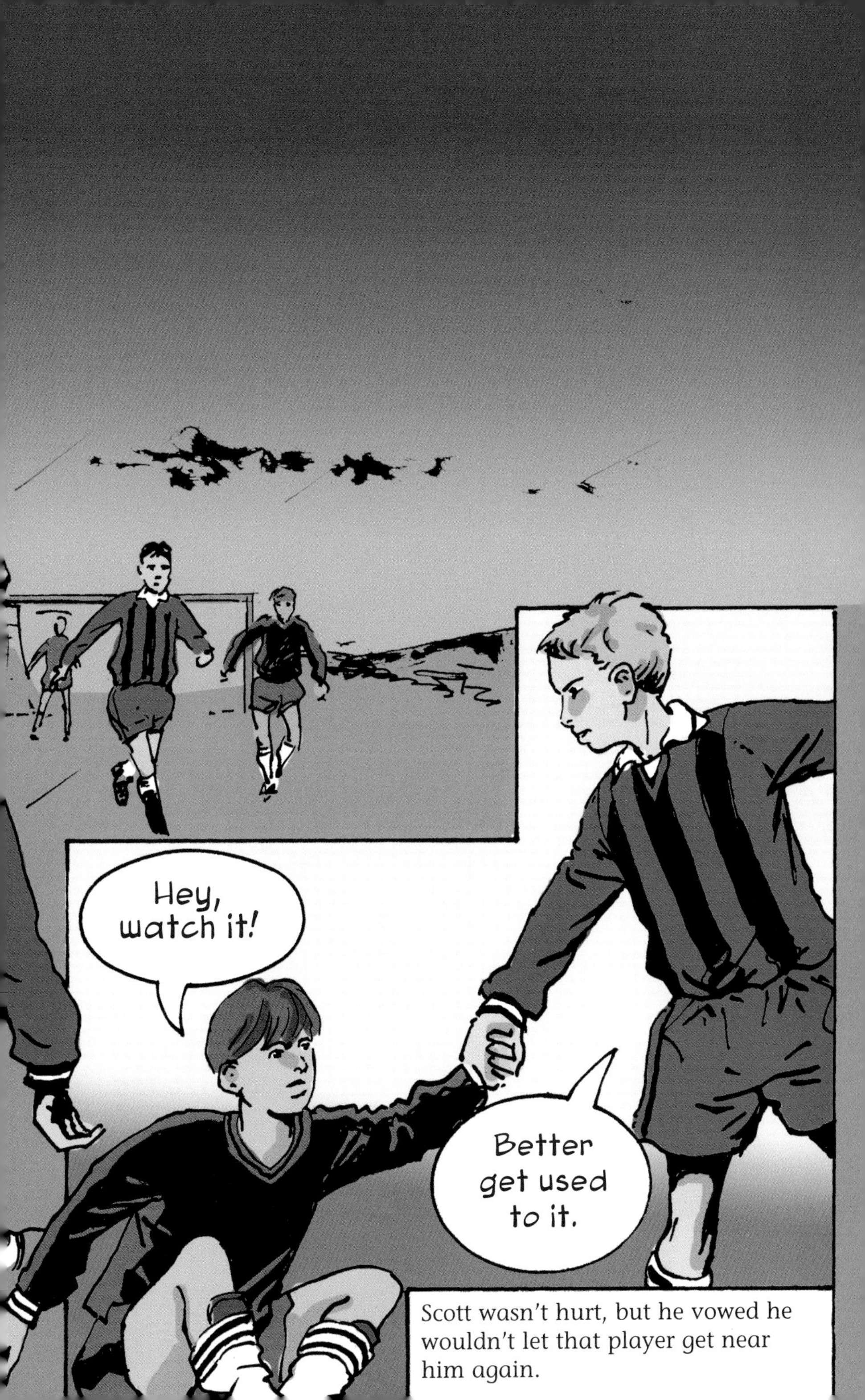
Hey, watch it!
Better get used to it.
Scott wasn't hurt, but he vowed he wouldn't let that player get near him again.

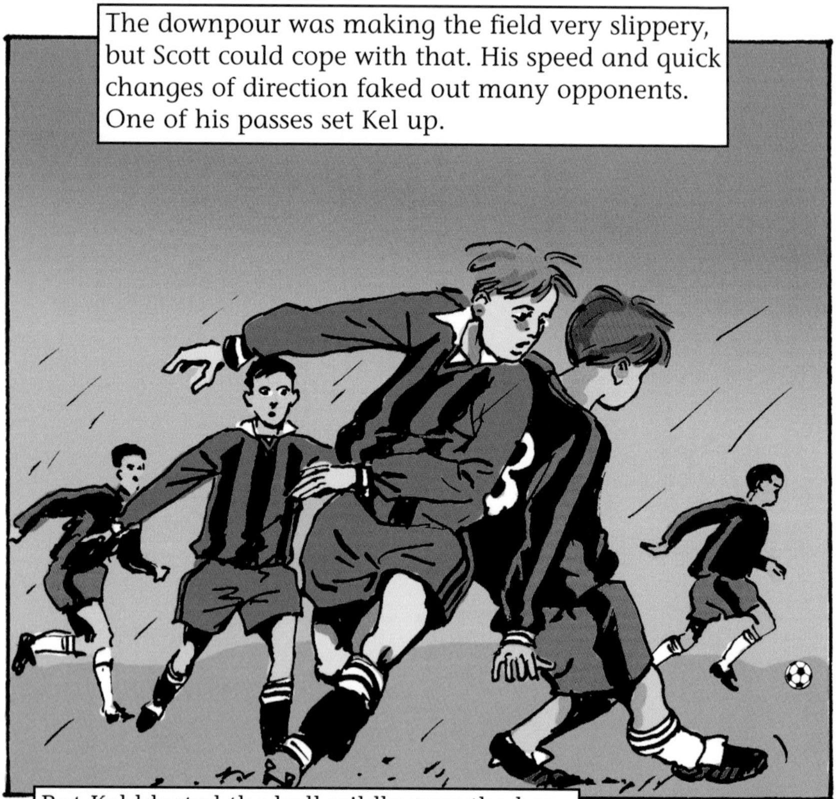
The downpour was making the field very slippery, but Scott could cope with that. His speed and quick changes of direction faked out many opponents. One of his passes set Kel up.

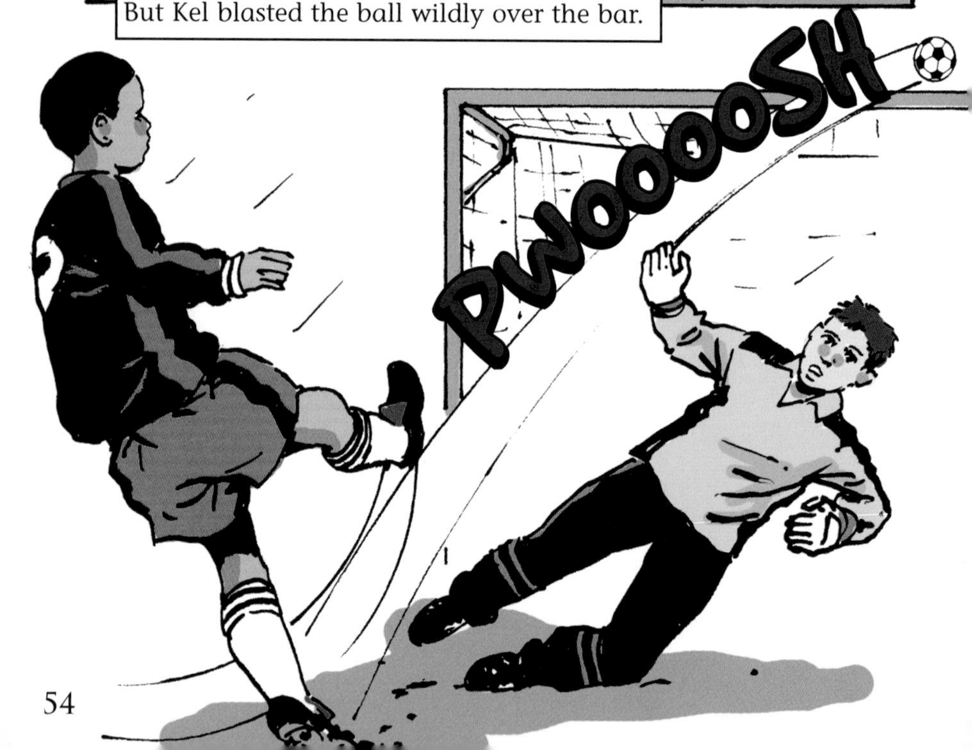
But Kel blasted the ball wildly over the bar.
PWOOOOOSH

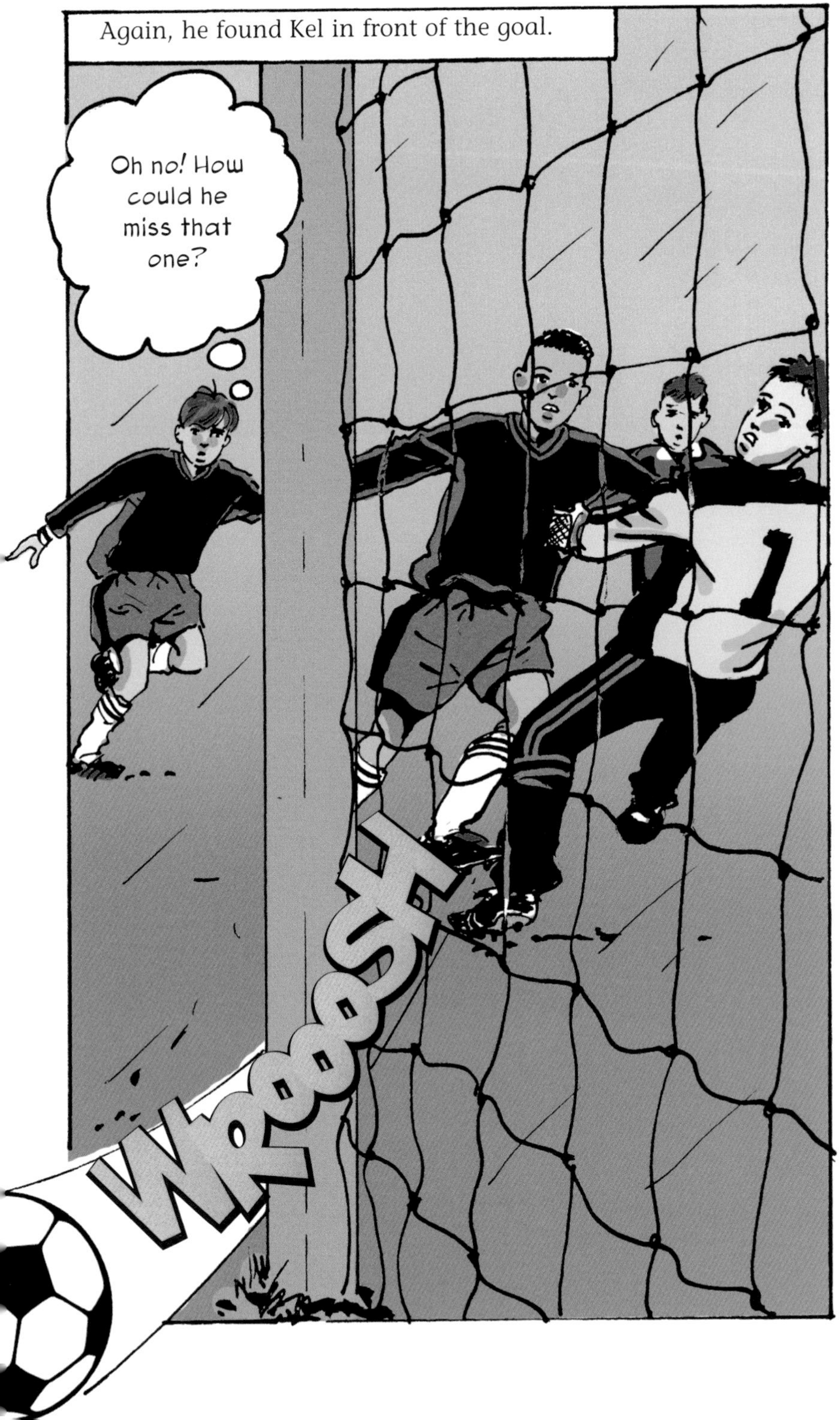
Again, he found Kel in front of the goal.
Oh no! How could he miss that one?
WROOOSH

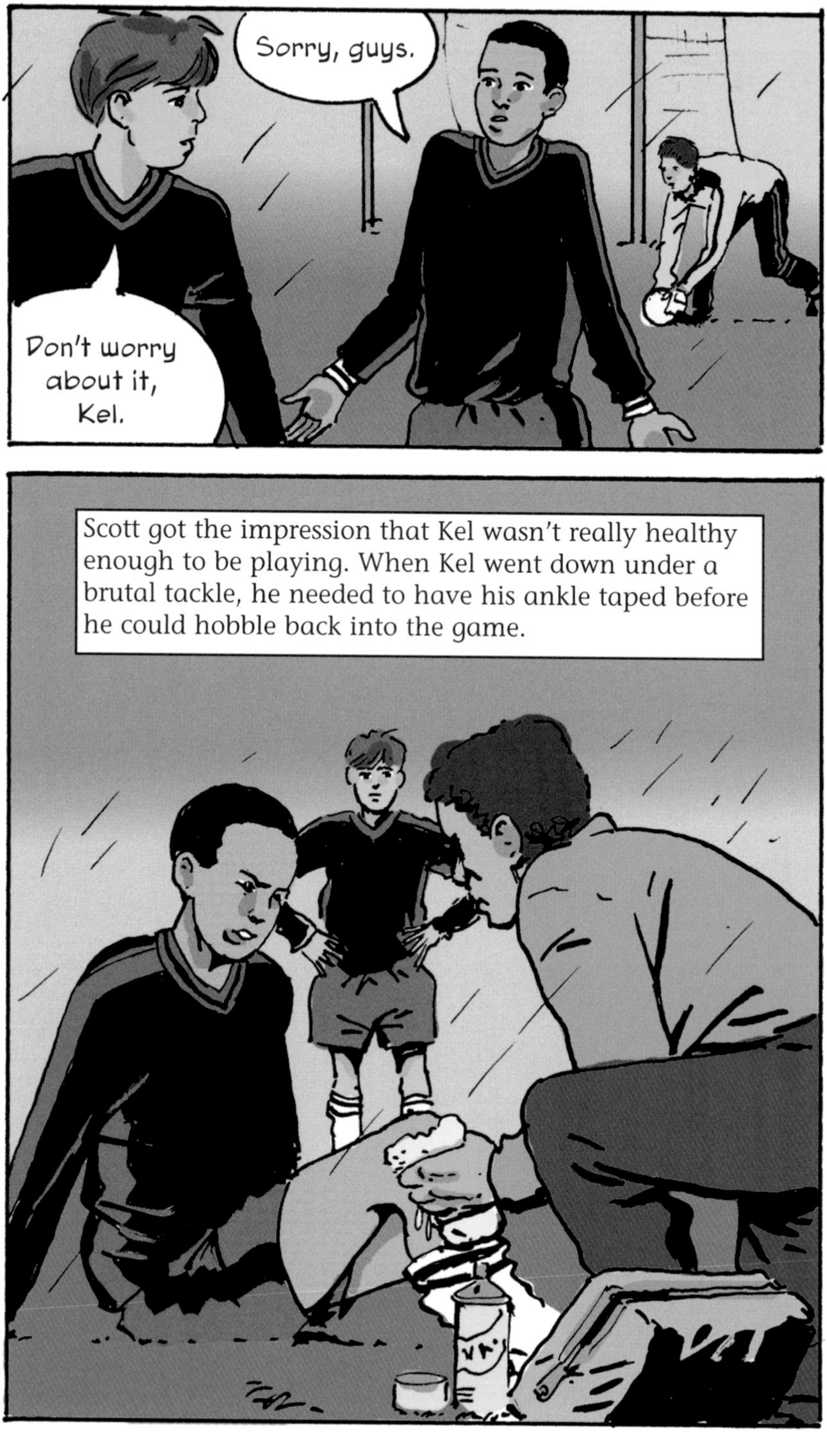
Sorry, guys.
Don't worry about it, Kel.
Scott got the impression that Kel wasn't really healthy enough to be playing. When Kel went down under a brutal tackle, he needed to have his ankle taped before he could hobble back into the game.

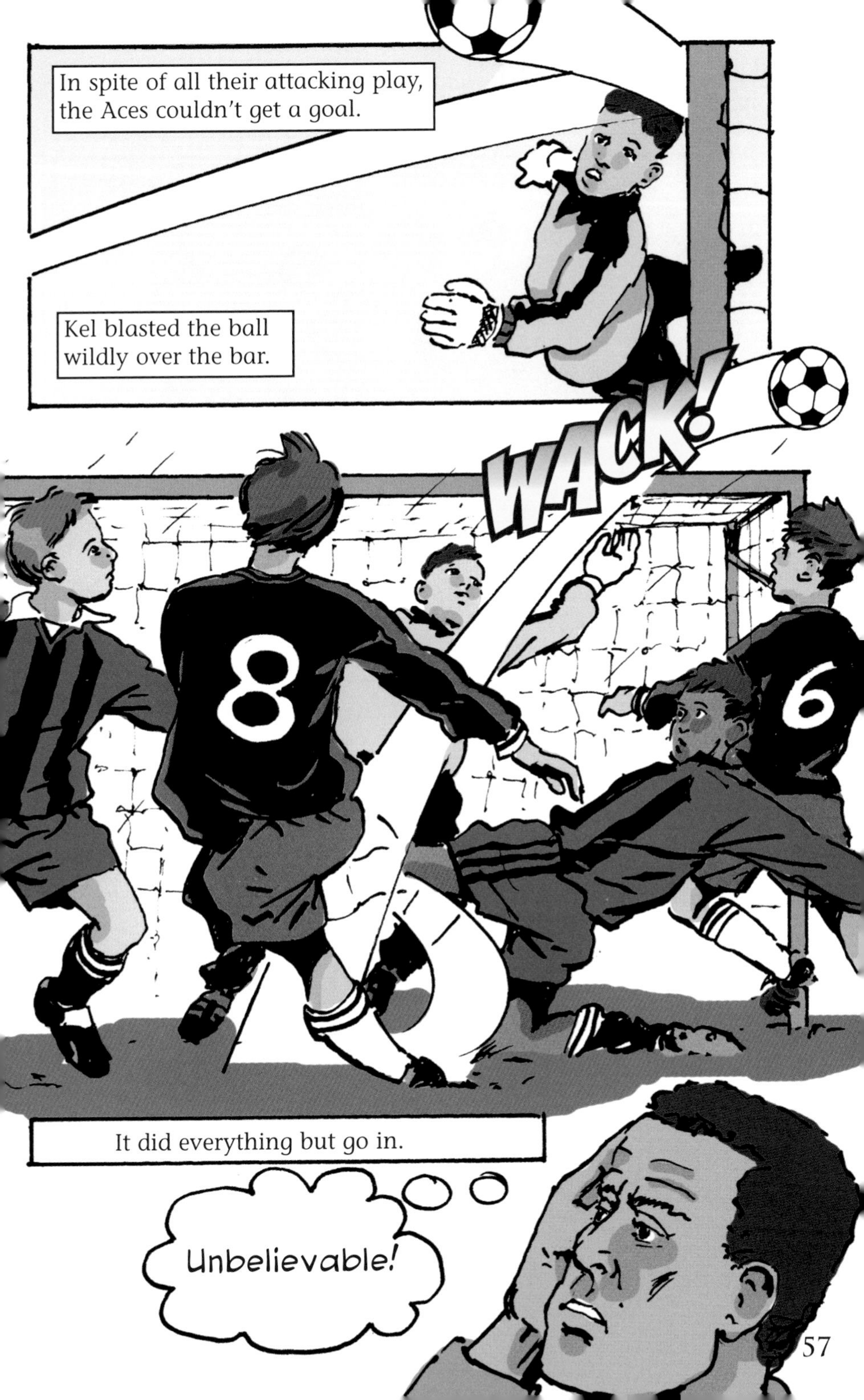
In spite of all their attacking play, the Aces couldn't get a goal.
Kel blasted the ball wildly over the bar.
WACK!
It did everything but go in.
Unbelievable!

Then Kel was fouled on the edge of the box. The free kick was taken quickly, and the Weather Hill defense was caught napping.

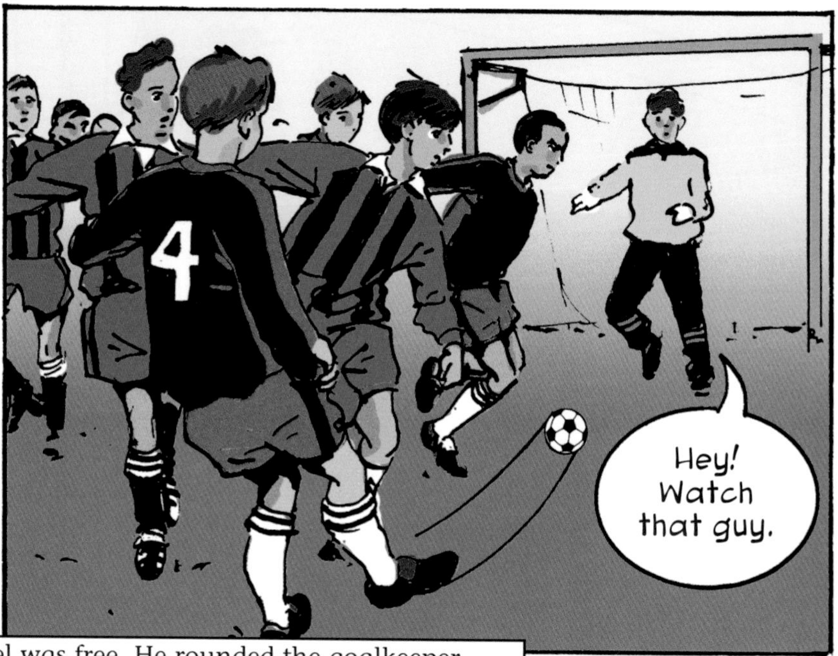
Hey! Watch that guy.

Kel was free. He rounded the goalkeeper . . .

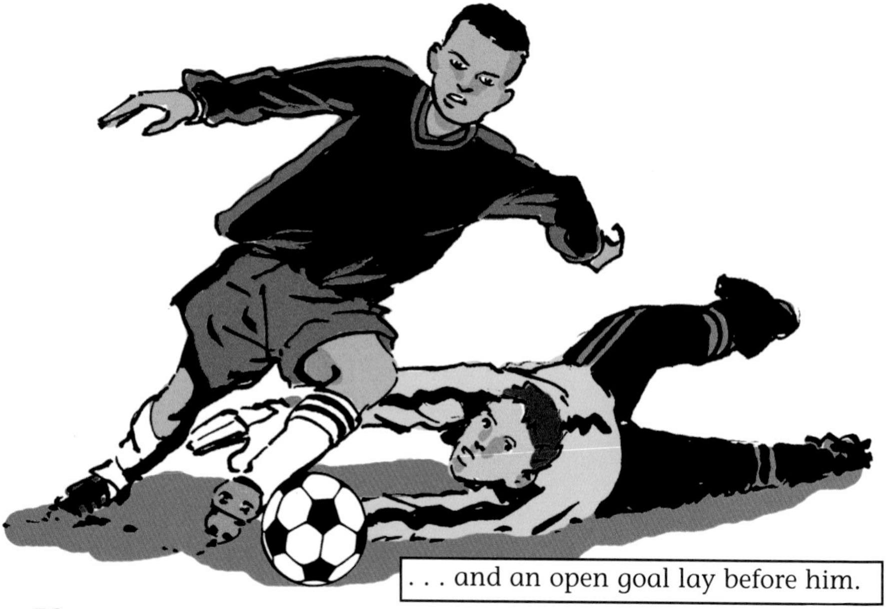

. . . and an open goal lay before him.

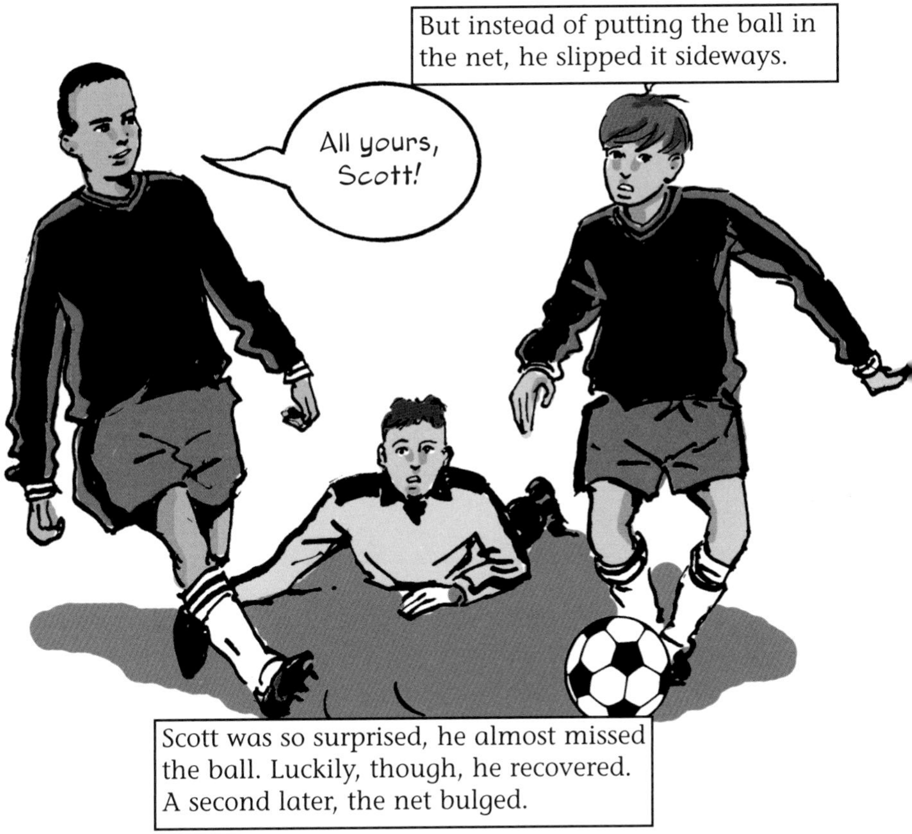
But instead of putting the ball in the net, he slipped it sideways.
All yours, Scott!
Scott was so surprised, he almost missed the ball. Luckily, though, he recovered. A second later, the net bulged.

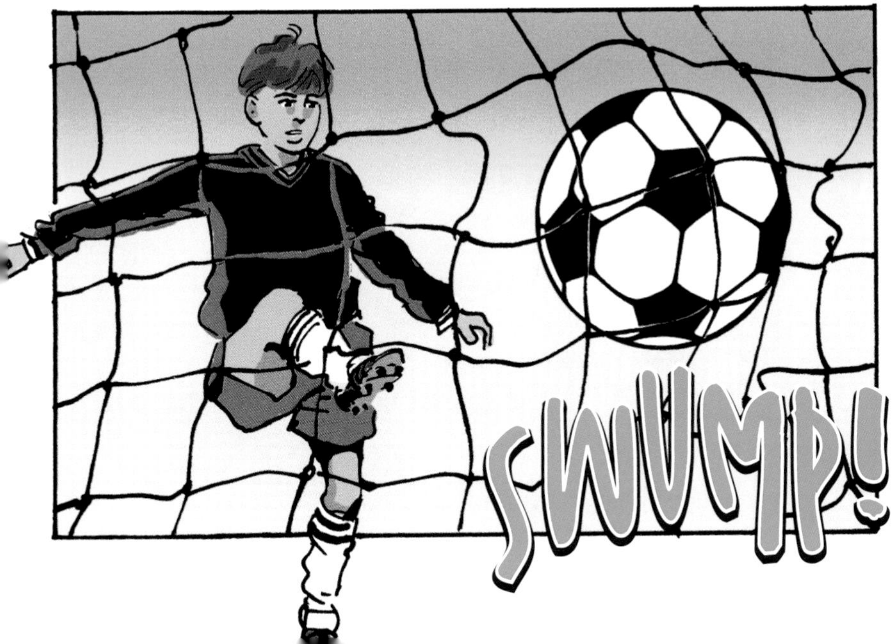
SWUMP!

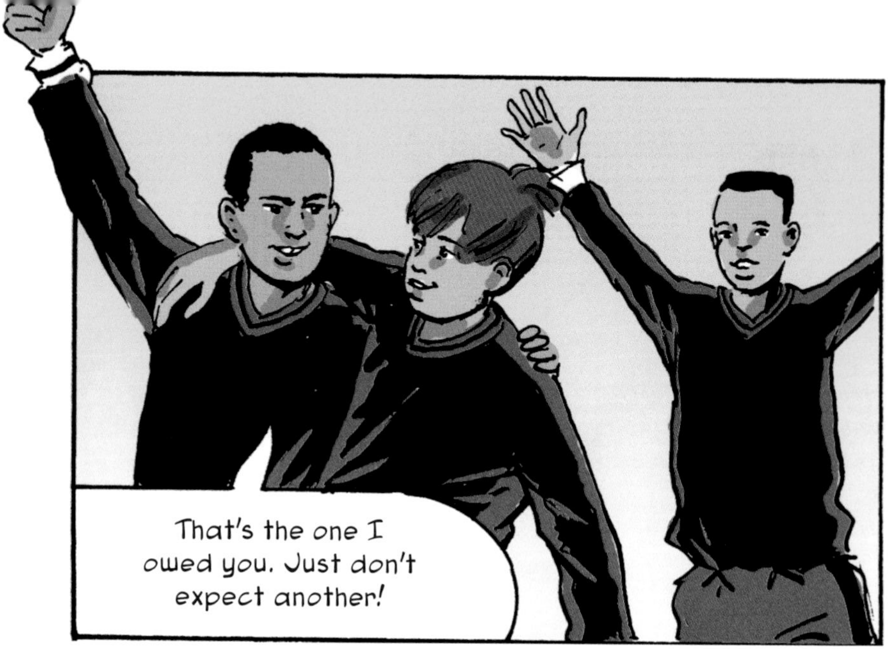
That's the one I owed you. Just don't expect another!

So the Aces won 1-0 to advance to the next game. If they hadn't, Coach told Kel, he would never have forgiven him. Kel wasn't really listening. His ankle injury flared up again.

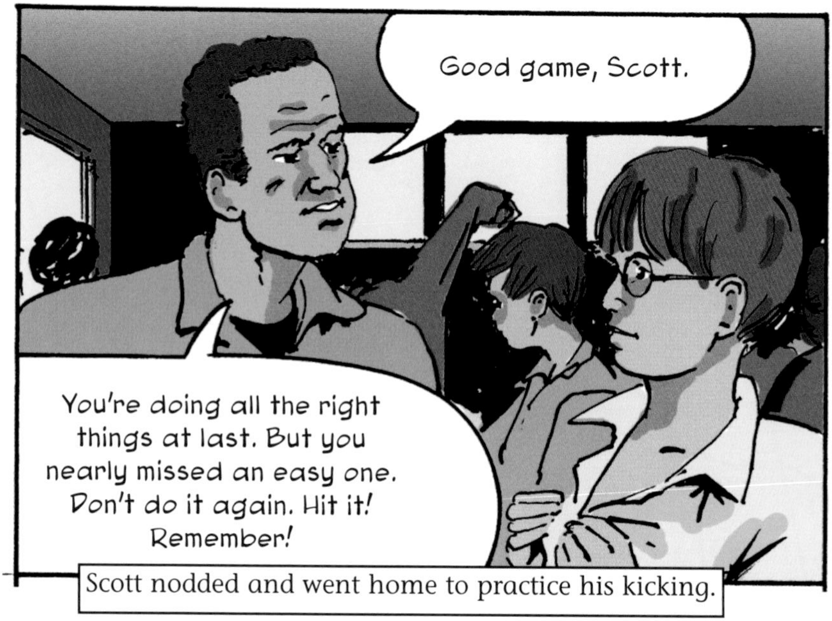
Good game, Scott.
You're doing all the right things at last. But you nearly missed an easy one. Don't do it again. Hit it! Remember!

Scott nodded and went home to practice his kicking.

CHAPTER SIX

At the last game of the season, the Aces needed just one point to win the league championship. Kel was the team's top-scorer. Scott was one goal behind him.

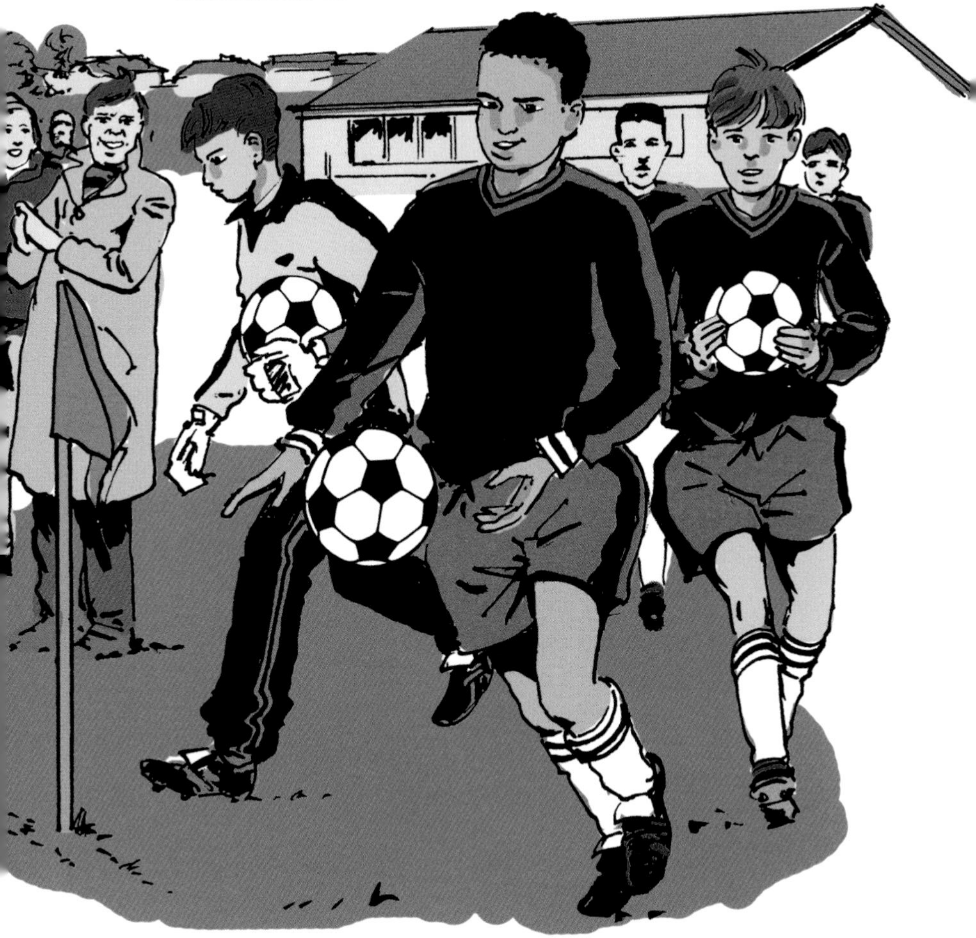

Kel still hadn't recovered from his ankle injury and had missed two games. Scott, his confidence increasing game by game, believed he could still snatch the trophy as the team's top scorer.

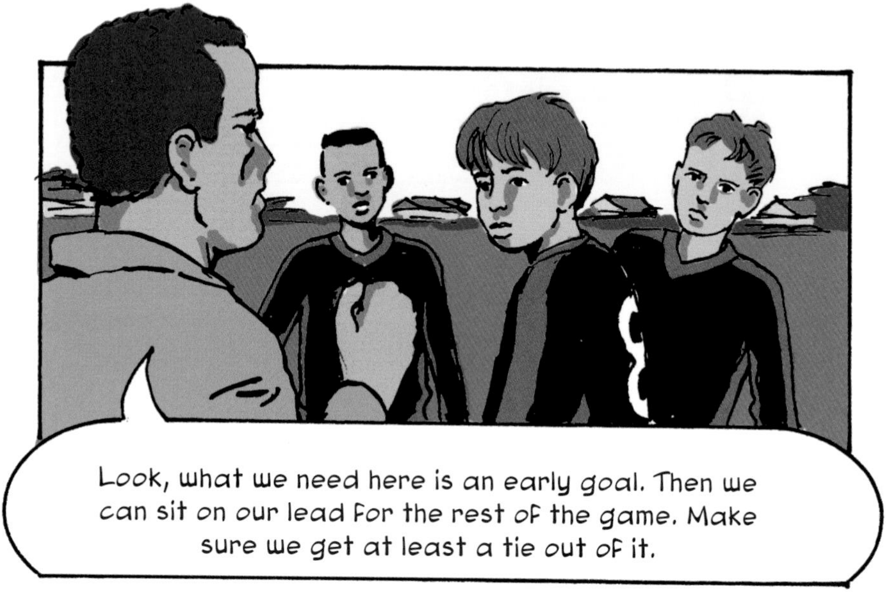
Look, what we need here is an early goal. Then we can sit on our lead for the rest of the game. Make sure we get at least a tie out of it.

As usual, defense dominated Coach Royce's thinking.

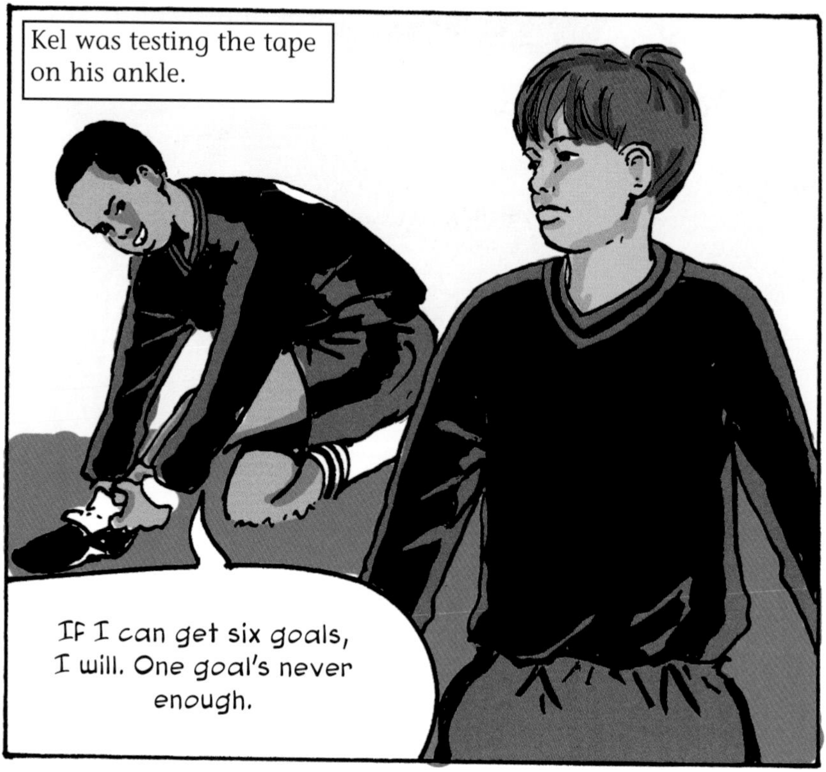
Kel was testing the tape on his ankle.
If I can get six goals, I will. One goal's never enough.

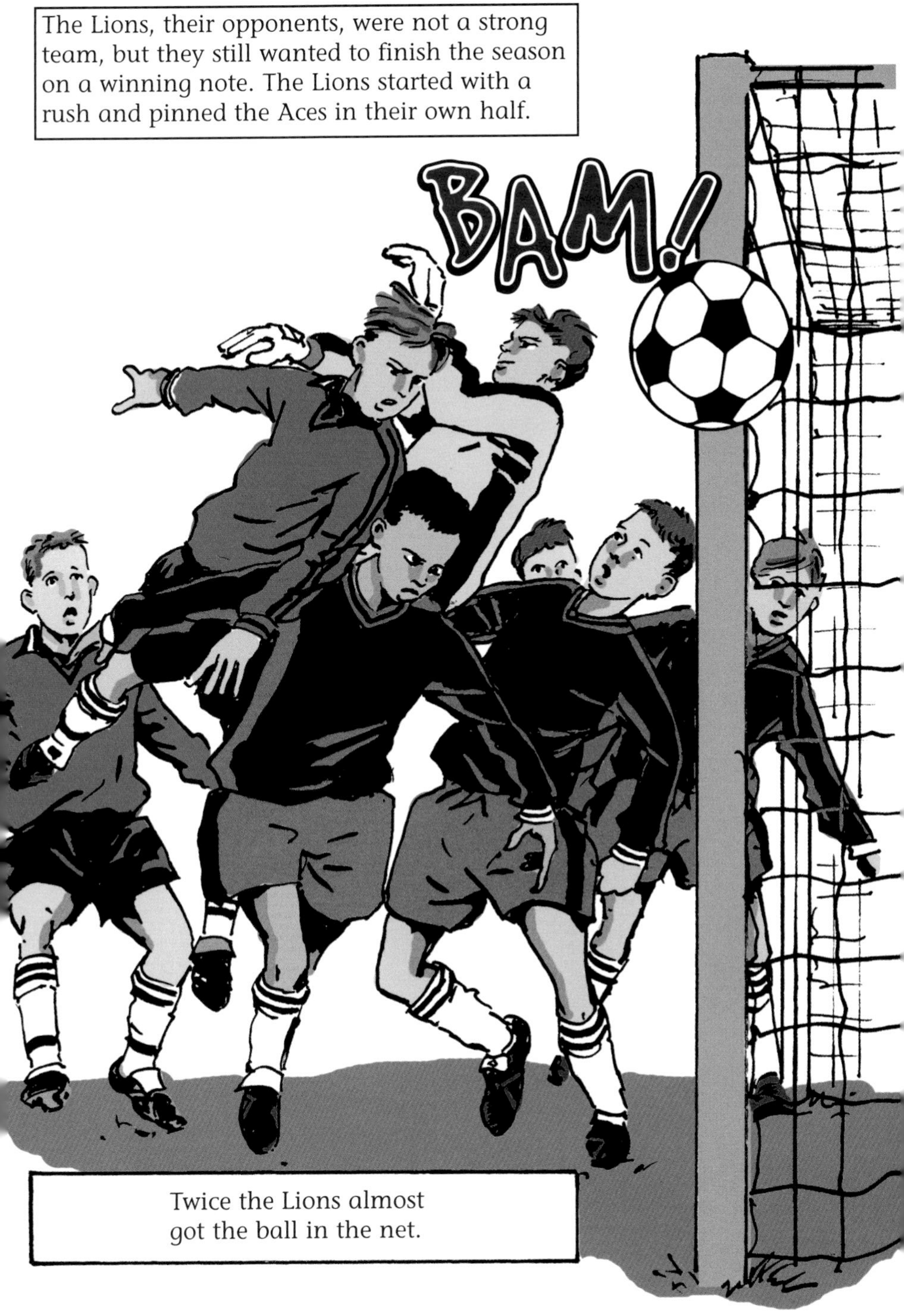
The Lions, their opponents, were not a strong team, but they still wanted to finish the season on a winning note. The Lions started with a rush and pinned the Aces in their own half.
BAM!
Twice the Lions almost got the ball in the net.

Coach was getting redder in the face by the second.

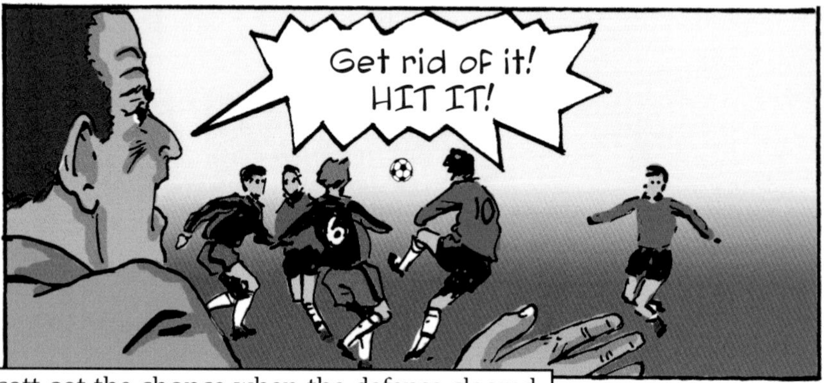
Get rid of it!
HIT IT!

Scott got the chance when the defense cleared the ball, and he picked it up midfield. As he ran, one opponent slipped on the soft ground, and another missed a tackle completely.

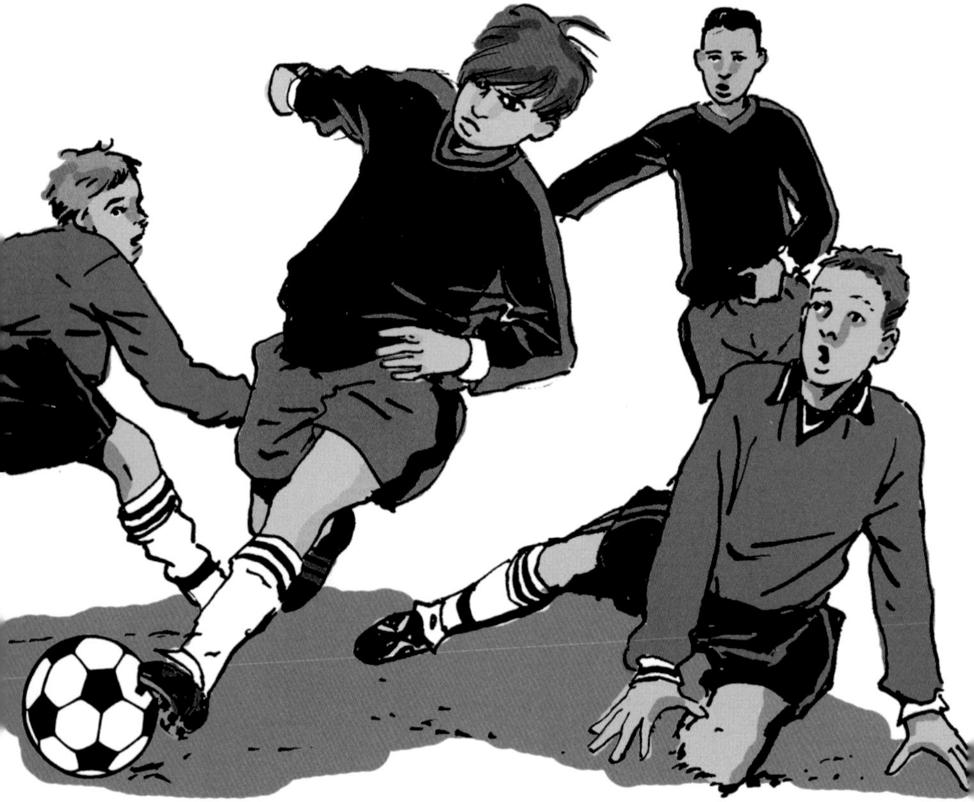

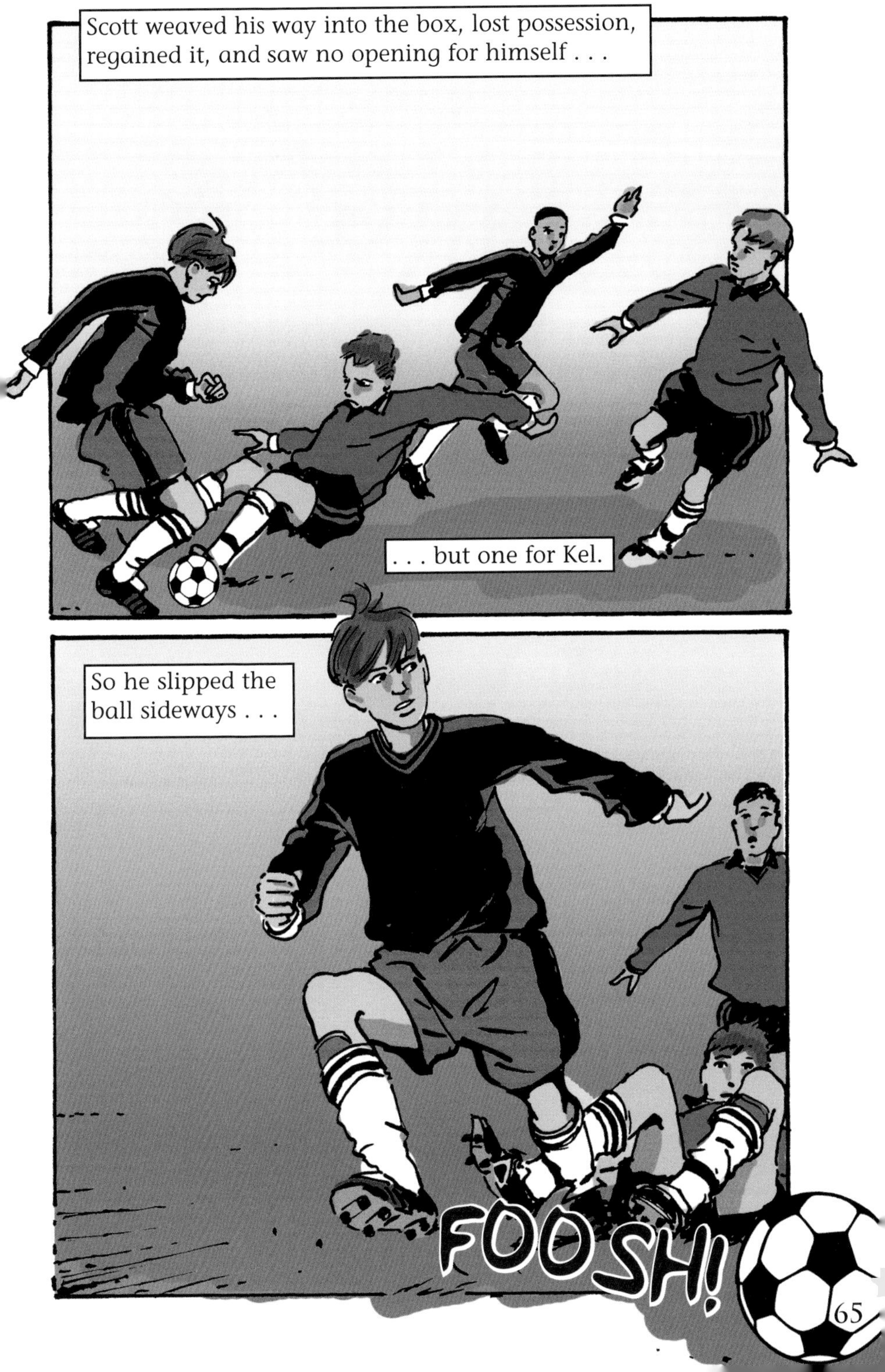

Scott weaved his way into the box, lost possession, regained it, and saw no opening for himself . . .
. . . but one for Kel.
So he slipped the ball sideways . . .
FOOSH!

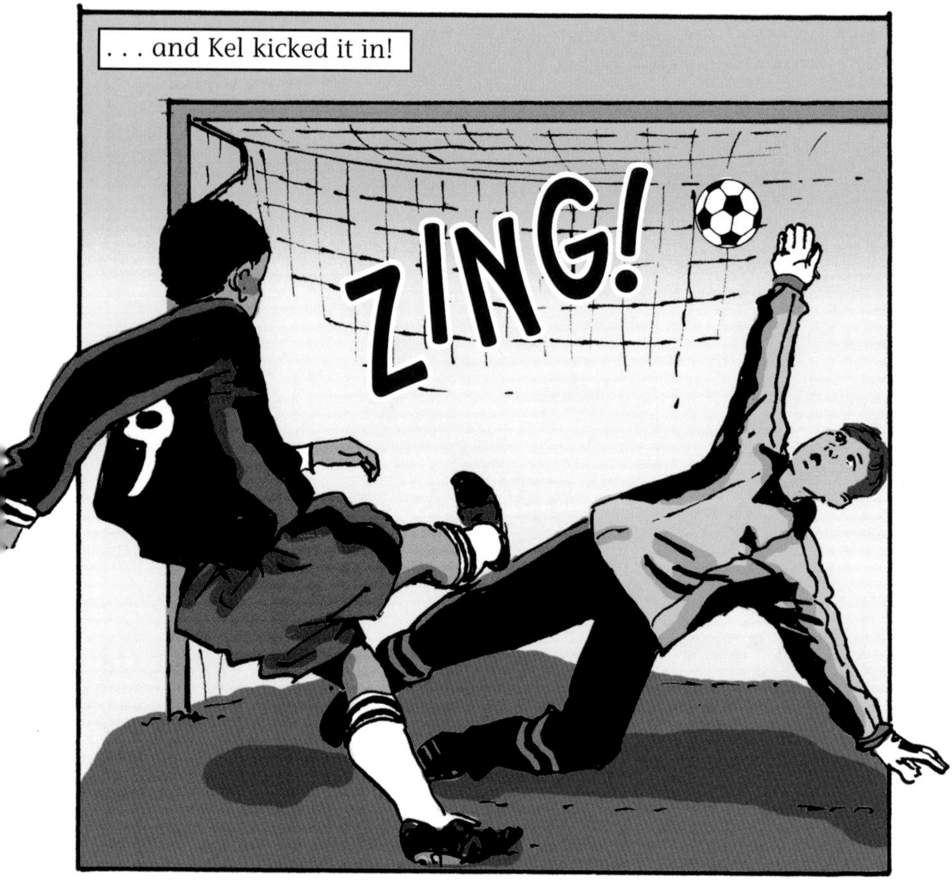
. . . and Kel kicked it in!
ZING!

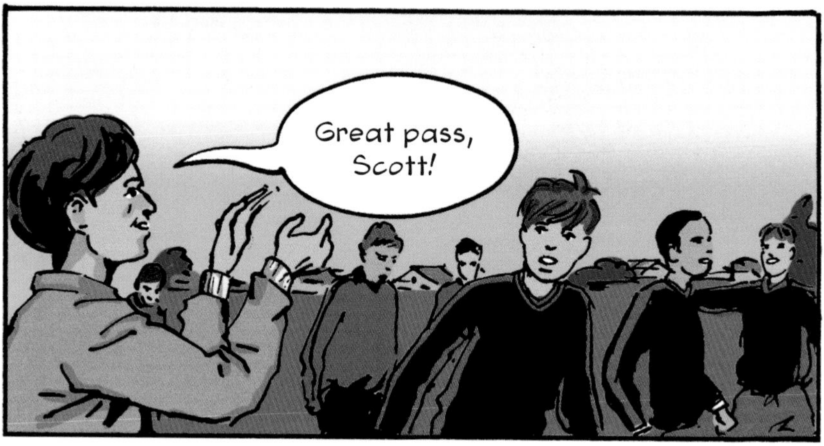
Great pass, Scott!

Ali stood on the sideline, cheering.

It was hard to tell who was happier, Coach Royce or Kel. Scott was happy for both of them. He knew now he had no real chance of taking the goal-scoring trophy, even though minutes later Kel limped off after another fierce knock on his ankle. The coach reorganized the defense, and Scott was ordered to stay back.

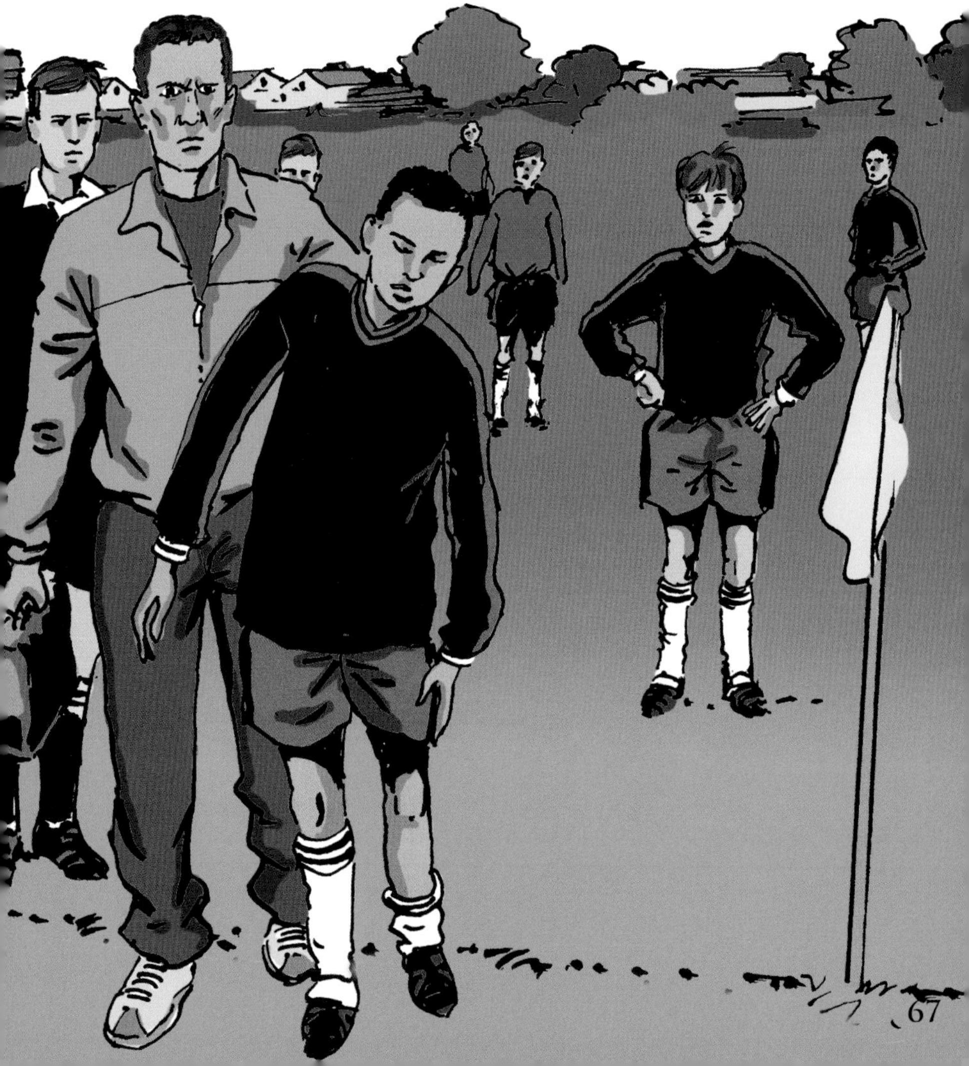

With the Aces' players staying back, the Lions were able to attack. Scott was running a lot but not enjoying it. His game was all about attacking, but the coach didn't allow that . . .

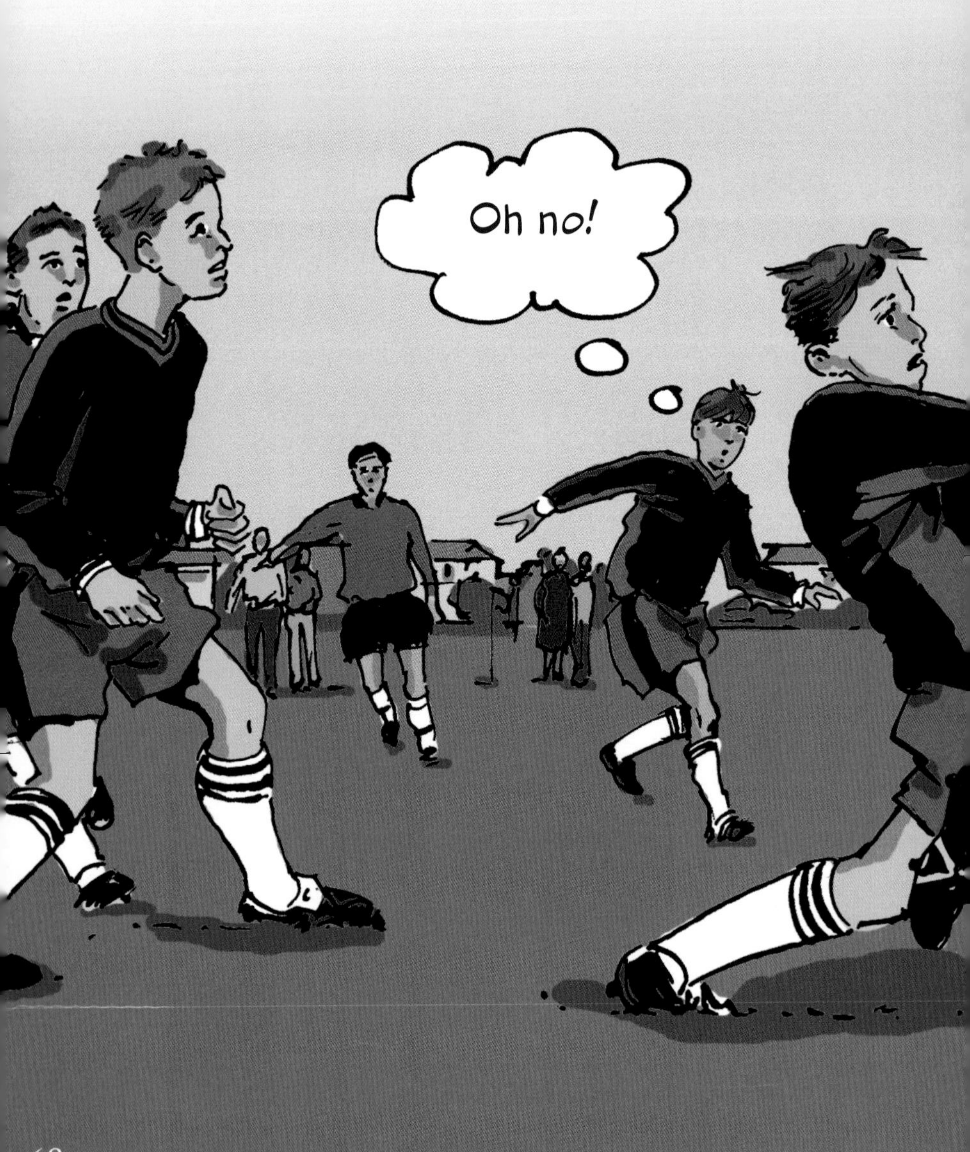
Oh no!

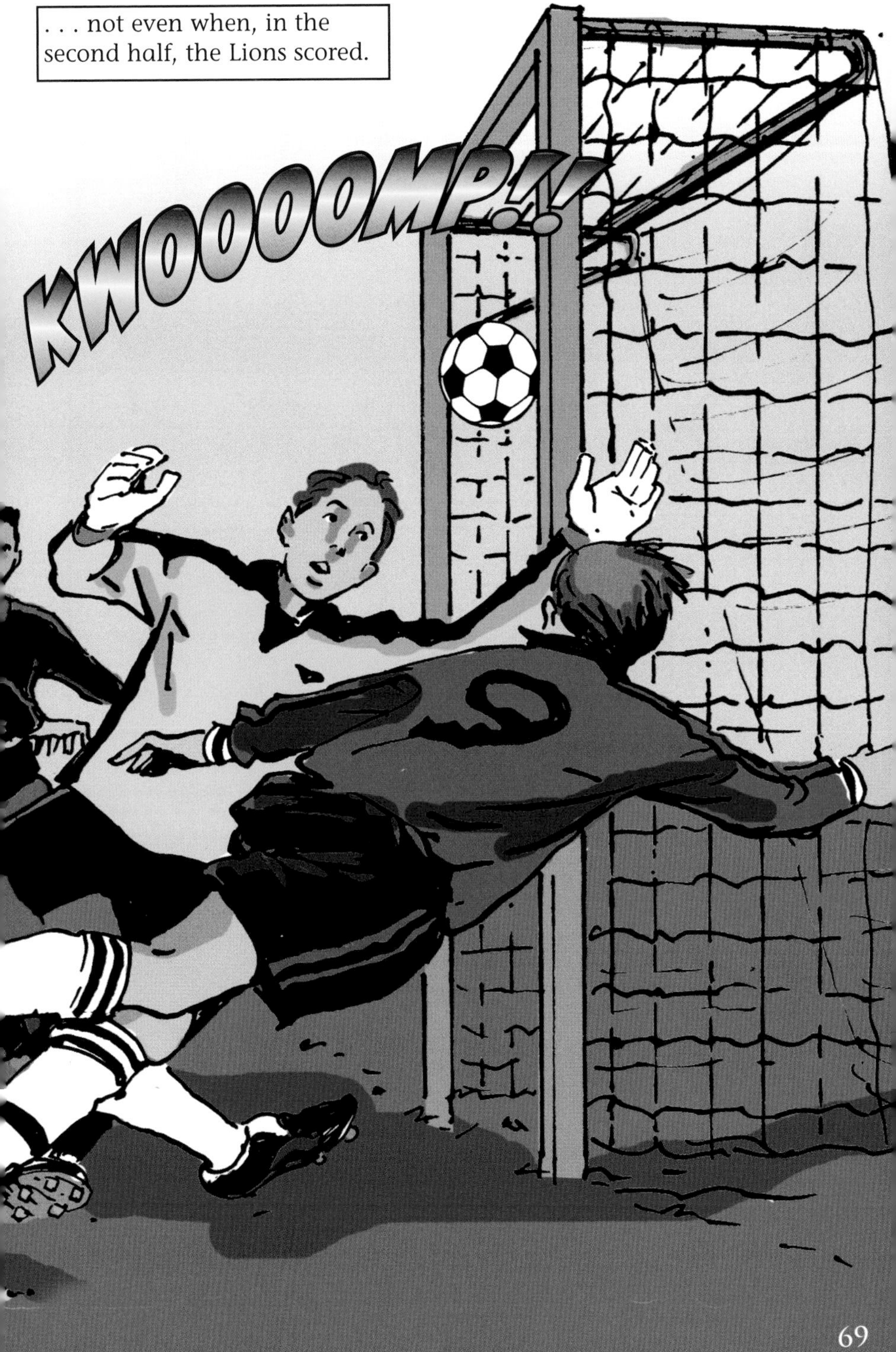

. . . not even when, in the second half, the Lions scored.
KWOOOOMP!!

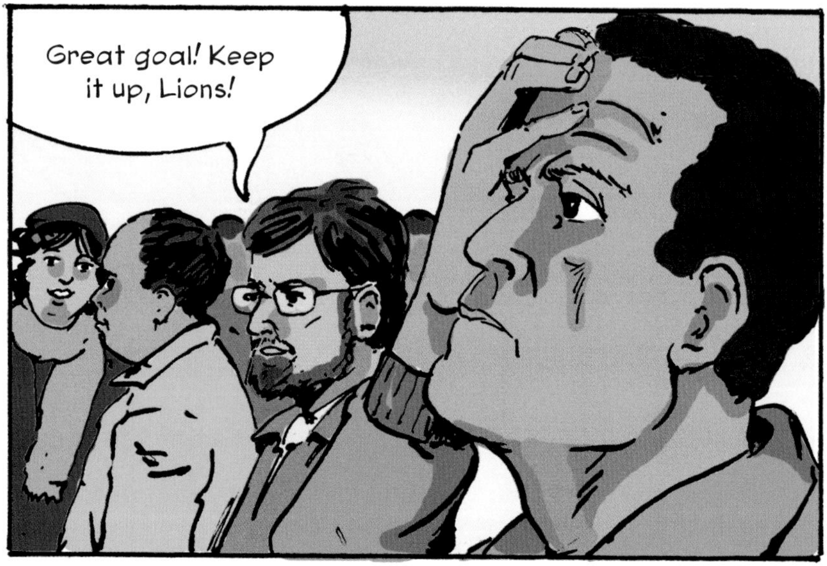
Great goal! Keep it up, Lions!

Time was running out.

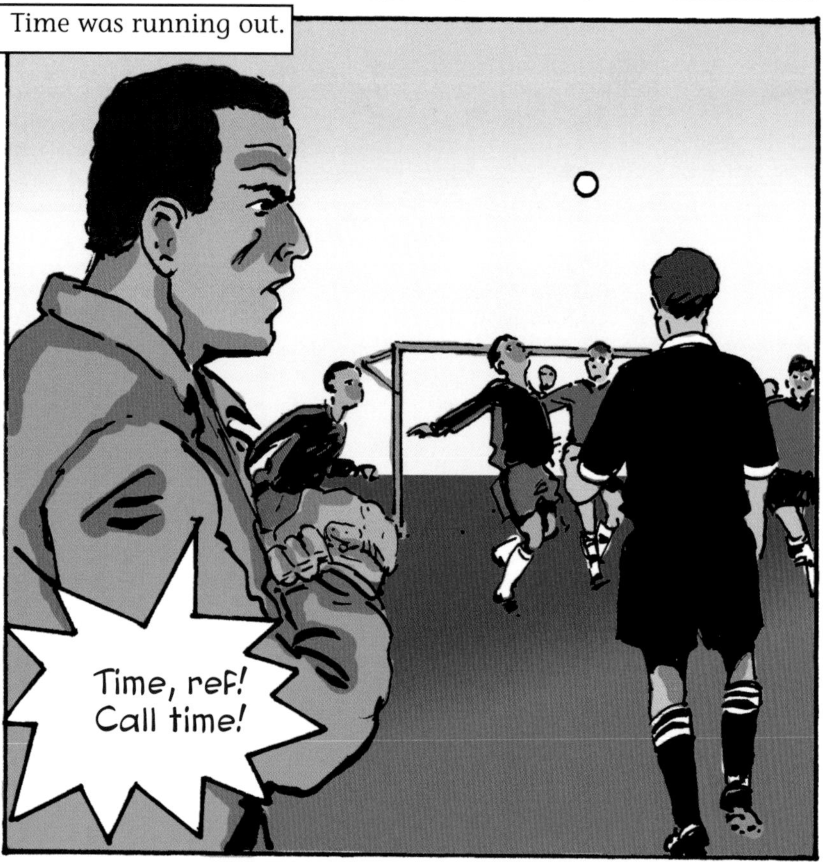
Time, ref! Call time!

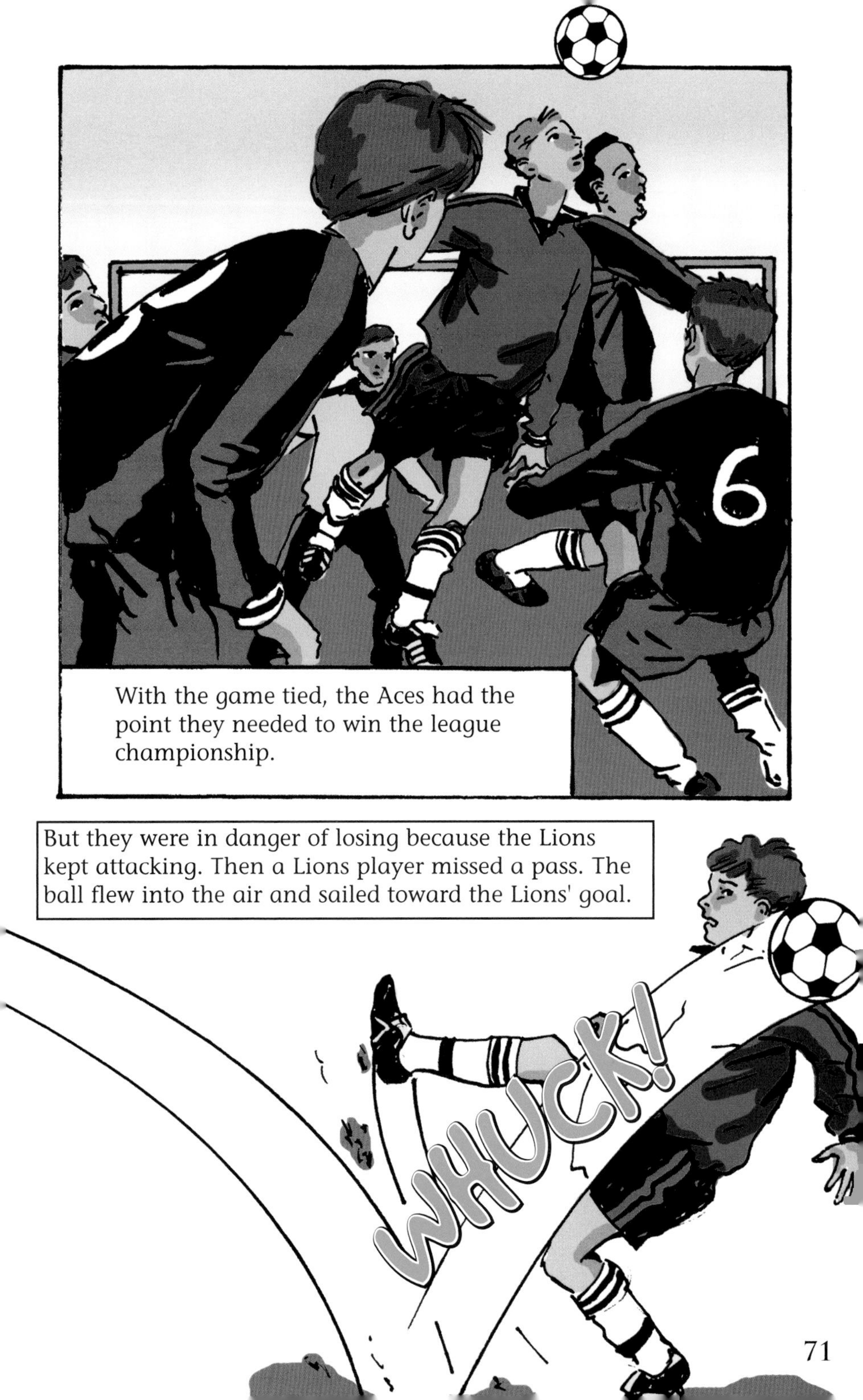
With the game tied, the Aces had the point they needed to win the league championship.
But they were in danger of losing because the Lions kept attacking. Then a Lions player missed a pass. The ball flew into the air and sailed toward the Lions' goal.
WHUCK!

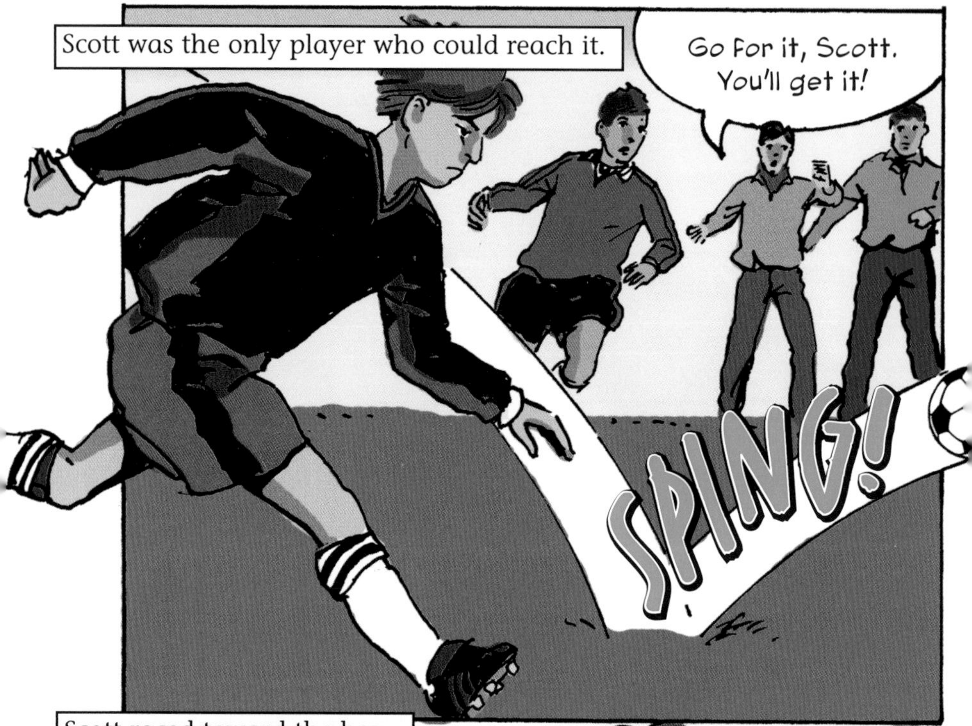
Scott was the only player who could reach it.
Go for it, Scott. You'll get it!
SPING!

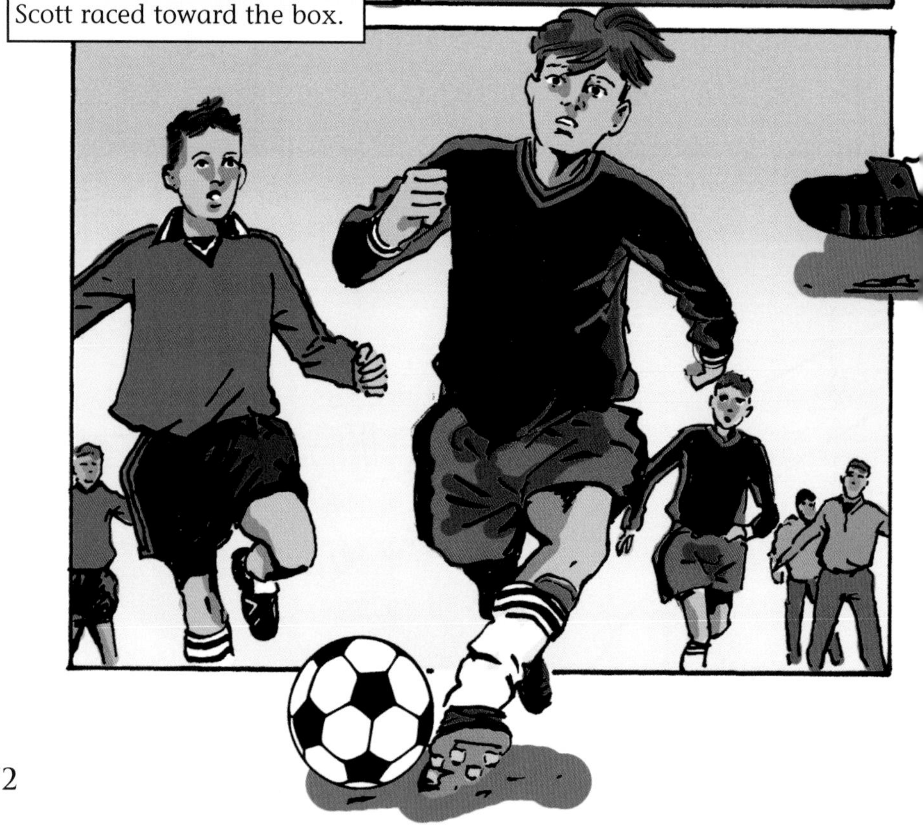
Scott raced toward the box.

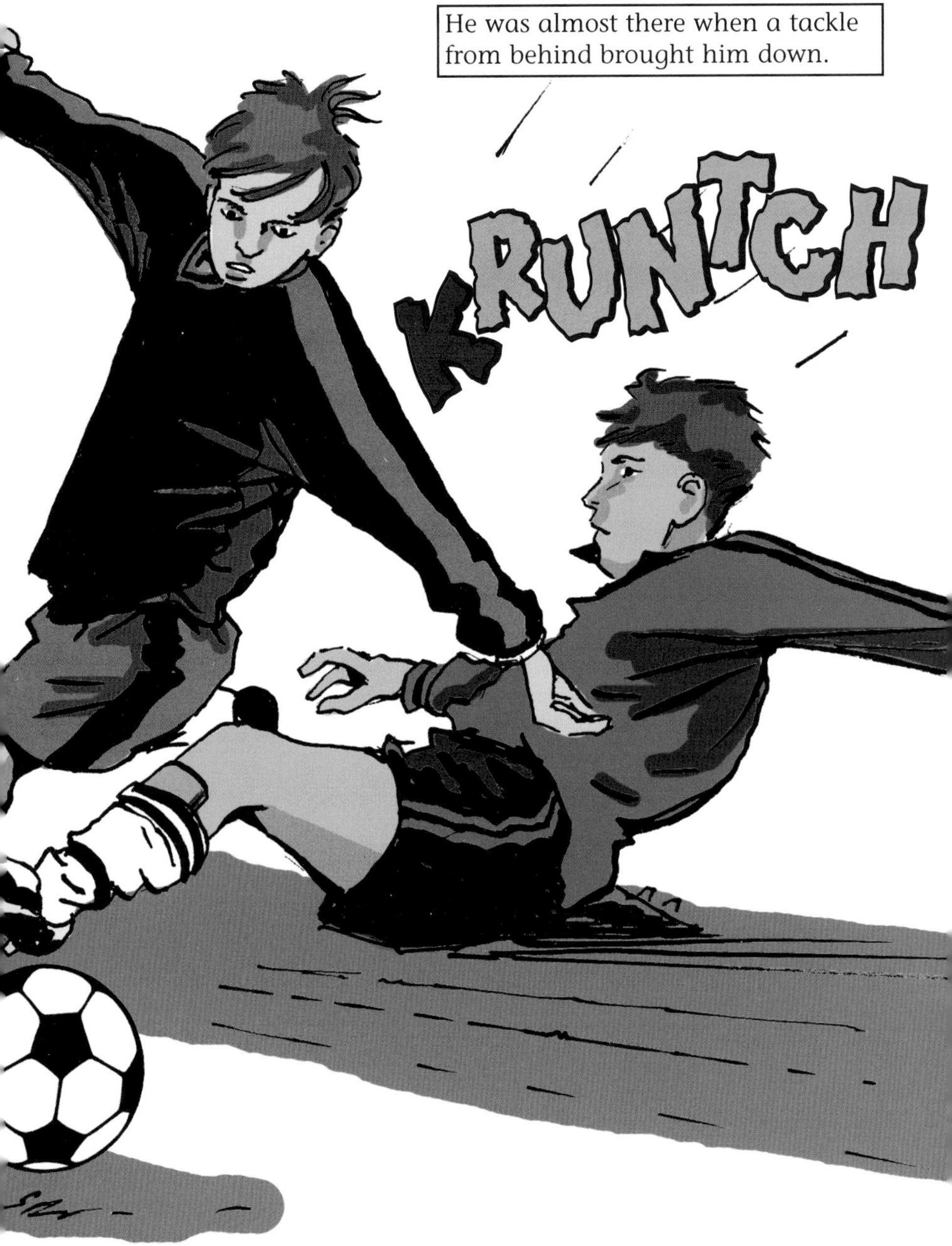
He was almost there when a tackle from behind brought him down.
KRUNTCH

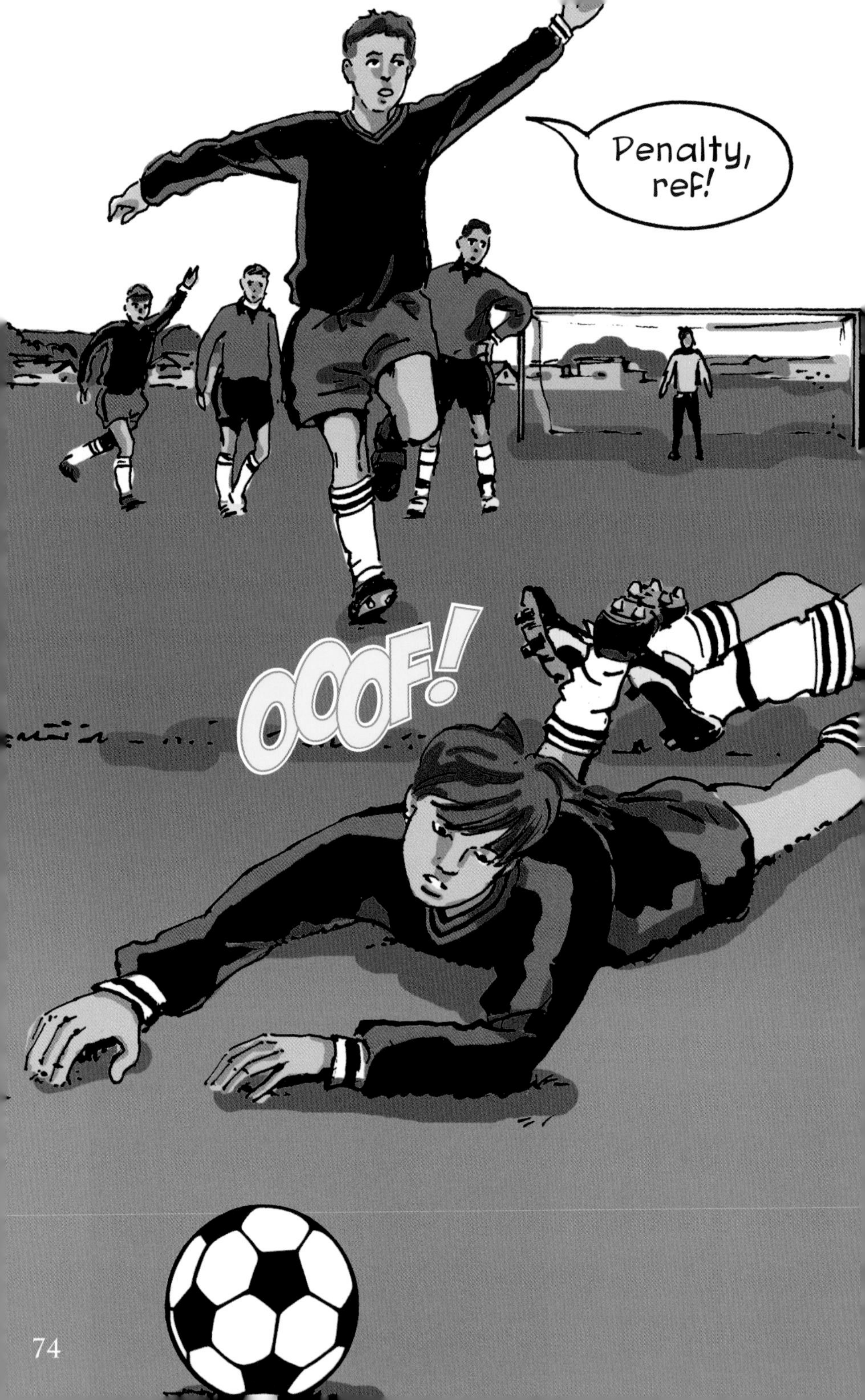
Penalty, ref!
OOOF!

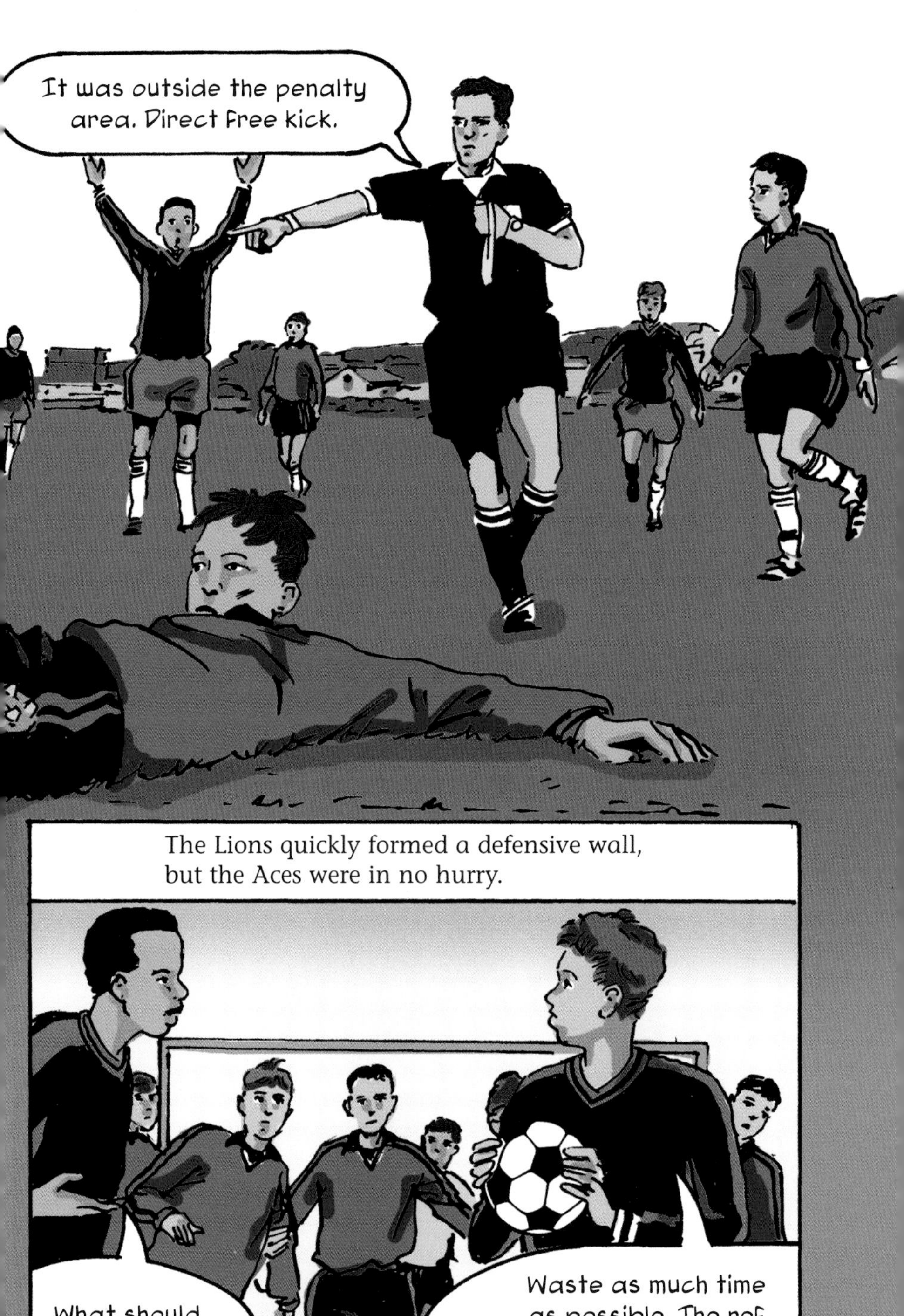
It was outside the penalty area. Direct free kick.
The Lions quickly formed a defensive wall, but the Aces were in no hurry.
What should we do?
Waste as much time as possible. The ref will call time soon.

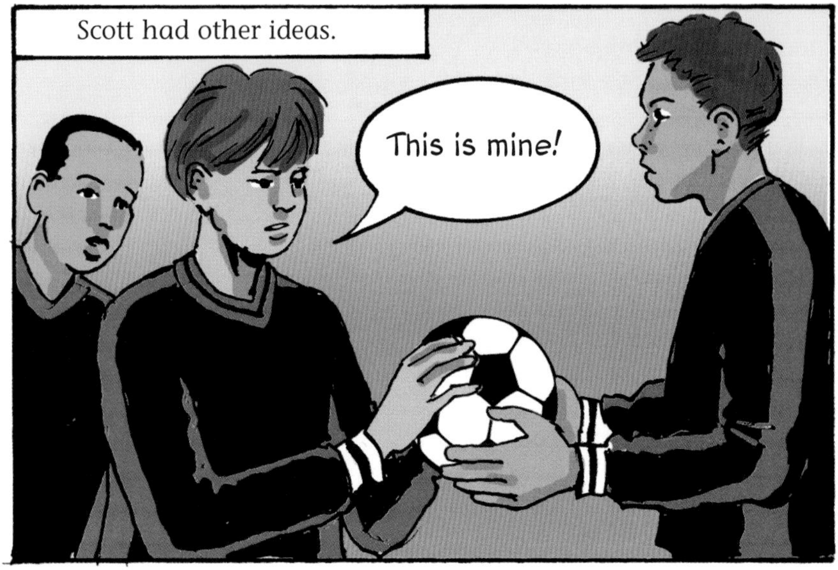
Scott had other ideas.
This is mine!

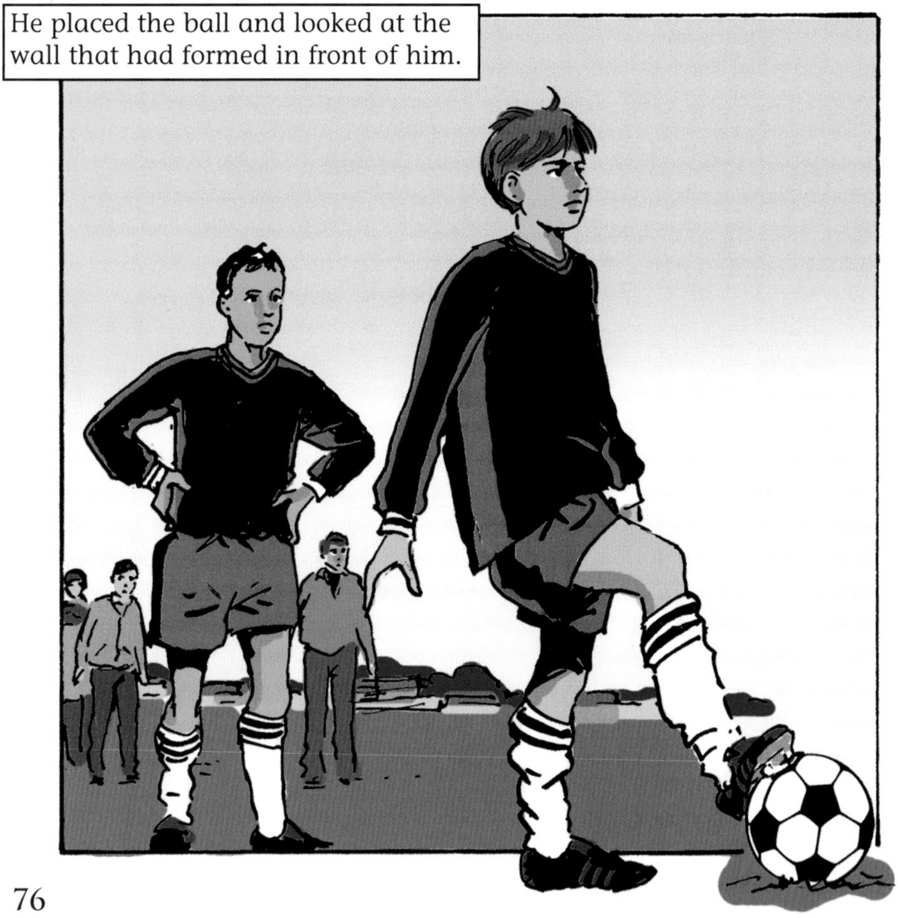
He placed the ball and looked at the wall that had formed in front of him.

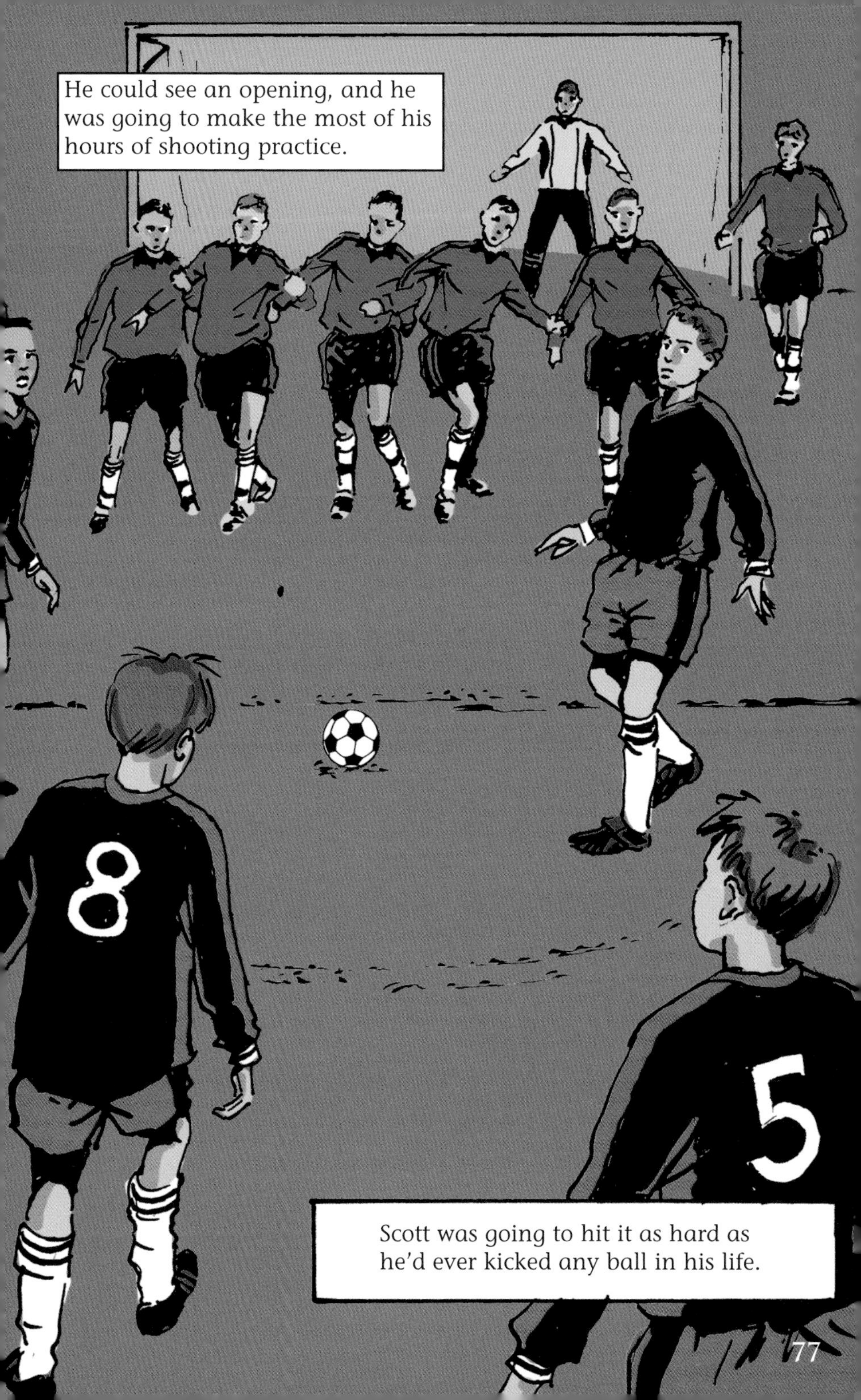
He could see an opening, and he was going to make the most of his hours of shooting practice.
8
5
Scott was going to hit it as hard as he'd ever kicked any ball in his life.

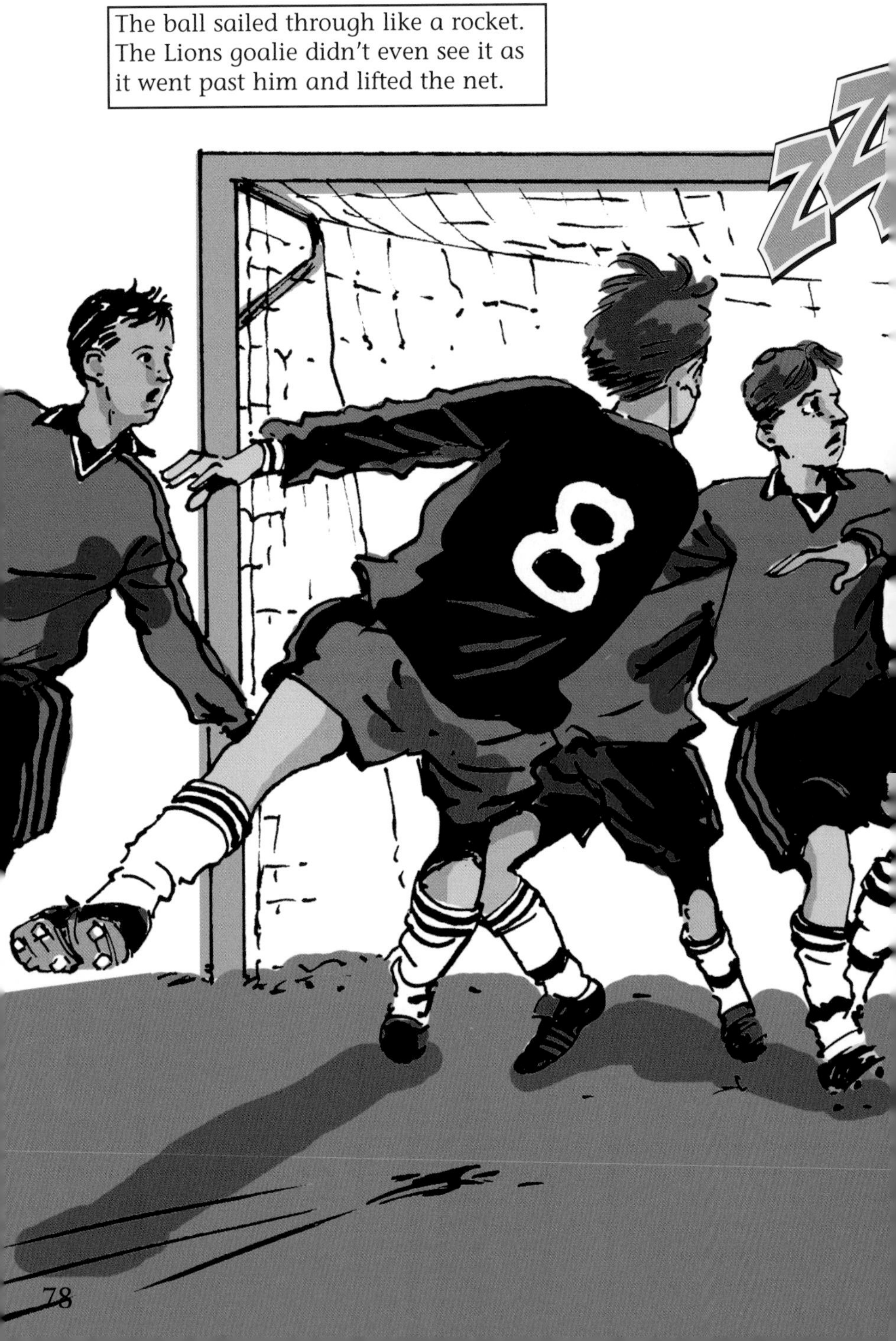
The ball sailed through like a rocket. The Lions goalie didn't even see it as it went past him and lifted the net.

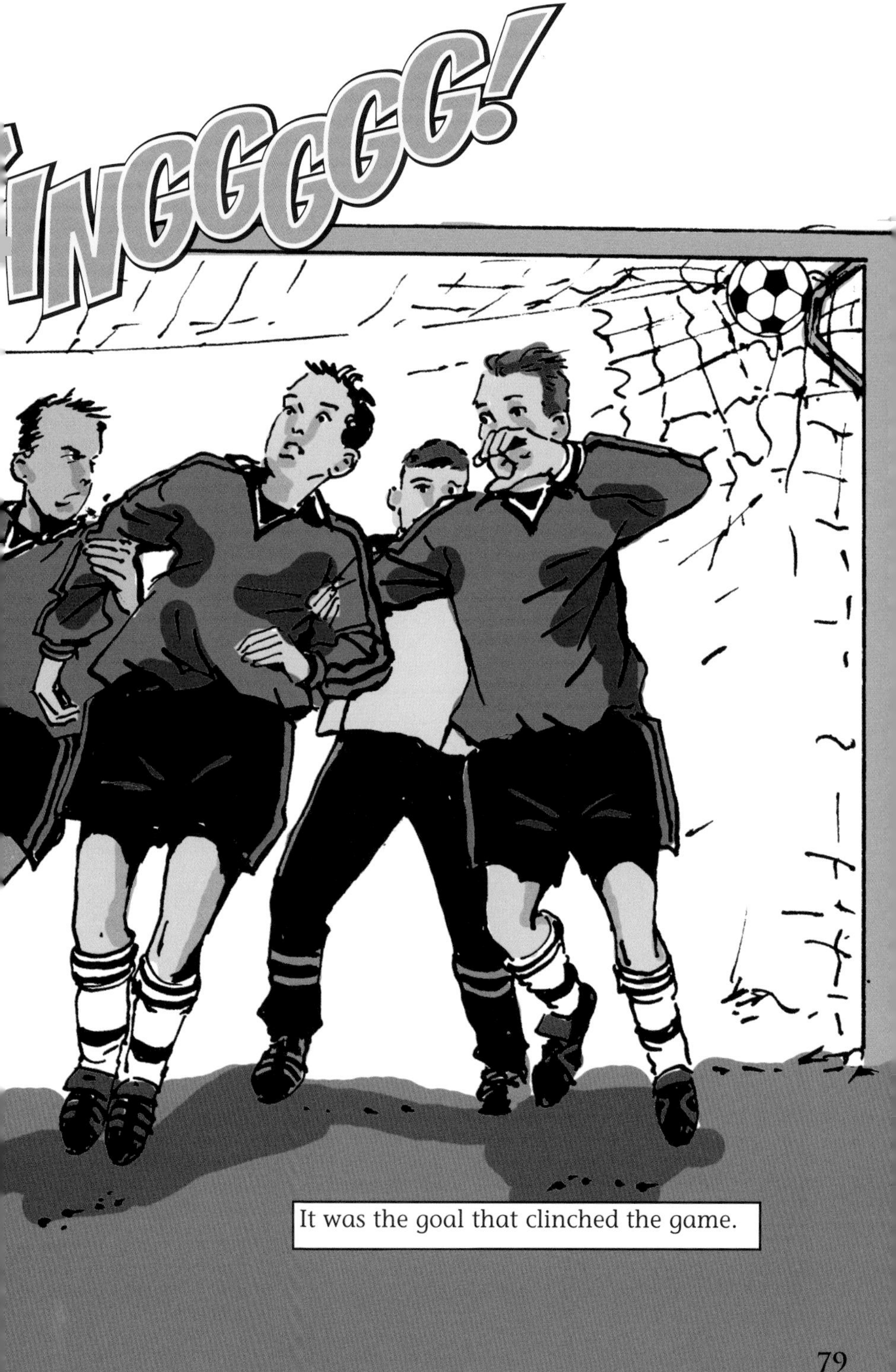
INGGGGG!
It was the goal that clinched the game.

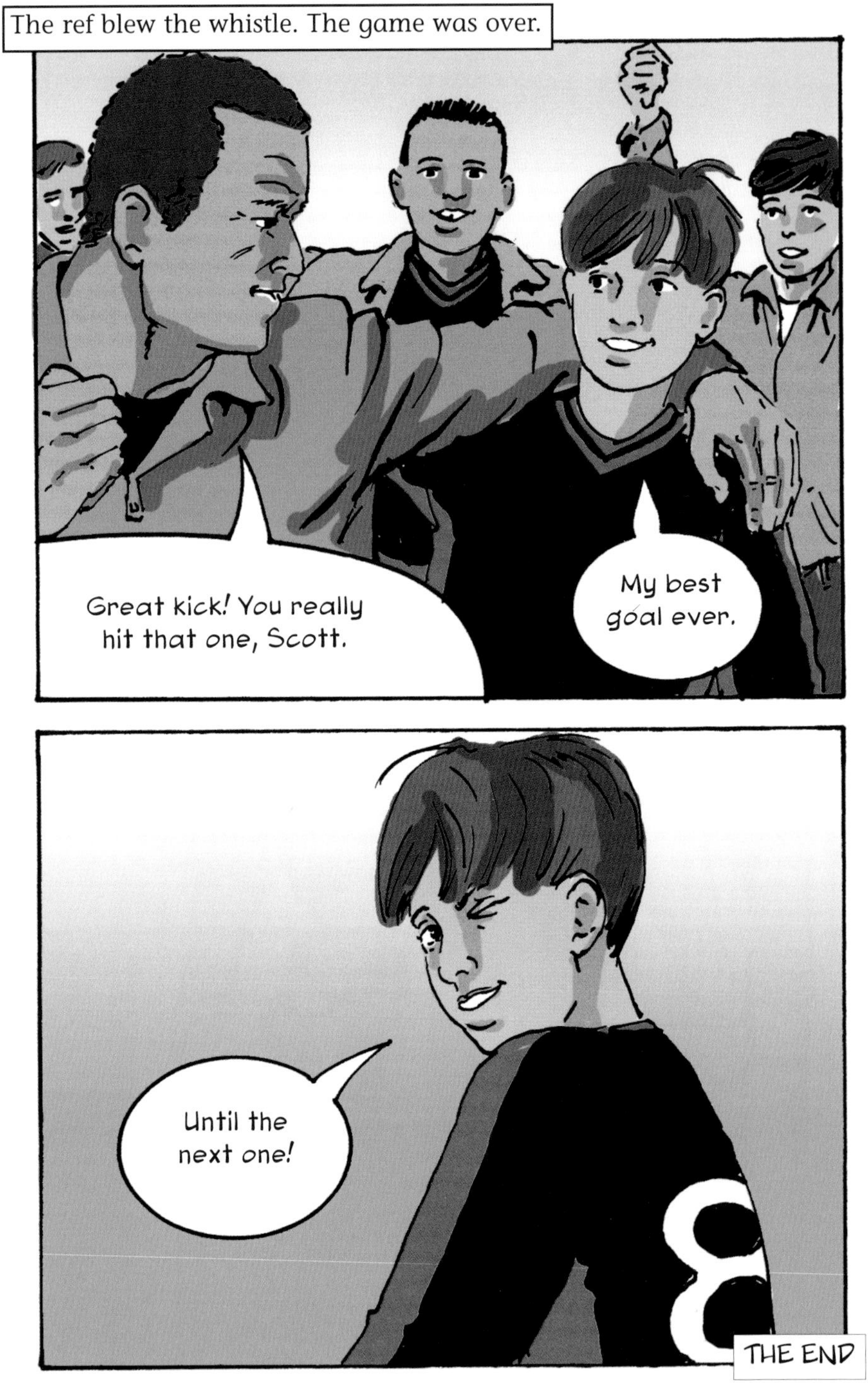
The ref blew the whistle. The game was over.
Great kick! You really hit that one, Scott.
My best goal ever.
Until the next one!
THE END

ABOUT THE AUTHOR

Michael Hardcastle loves sports. He enjoys playing them and writing about them — especially soccer. Michael has written more than 90 books on sports.

When he's not writing, Michael visits colleges and schools all over Great Britain to talk about his books and writing. He lives with his wife in Beverly, Yorkshire, Great Britain.

GLOSSARY

aggression (UH-gresh-uhn)—forceful behavior

brutal (BROO-tuhl)—to be cruel

ethic (EHTH-ik)—how people behave and react while performing their work; people with strong work ethics believe in hard work.

frantic (FRAN-tik)—fast, nervous action

opponent (uh-POH-nuhnt)—someone who plays against you in a game or sport

rival (RYE-vuhl)—a person you compete against

stamina (STAM-uh-nuh)—the ability to do something for a long period of time

vow (VOW)—a promise

INTERNET SITES

Do you want to know more about subjects related to this book? Or are you interested in learning about other topics? Then check out FactHound, a fun, easy way to find Internet sites.

Our investigative staff has already sniffed out great sites for you!

Here's how to use FactHound:

1. Visit *www.facthound.com*

2. Select your grade level.

3. To learn more about subjects related to this book, type in the book's ISBN number: **1598890271**.

4. Click the **Fetch It** button.

FactHound will fetch the best Internet sites for you.

DISCUSSION QUESTIONS

1. After stealing the ball from Scott and scoring a goal, Kel said "We're going to win this game, and that's what counts." Was he right or did Scott have a right to be mad at Kel?

2. Scott wasn't happy with the way he was playing soccer. What did he do to improve his play? How could you improve at the sports you play?

3. After all the mean things Kel said and did to Scott, why did Scott help Kel's sick dog?

4. During the last game, Scott's team was tied with the Lions and would win the league championship. Scott was told to stay back by his coach and let time run out, but he ran up to kick the ball when the Lions misplayed it. Why do you think he did this? Was it the right thing to do?

WRITING PROMPTS

1. Scott helped Kel with his dog even after Kel treated him poorly. Write about a time you decided to be nice to someone who wasn't nice to you. What did you do?

2. Scott disobeyed his coach's orders to stay back during the last few minutes of the final game, but he was able to score another goal. Imagine that you are Scott's coach. Write about what you would say to Scott at the end of the game.

3. Scott worked hard to be his team's top scorer. Even though he failed to achieve his goal, he was happy about how he played. Write about a time when you worked hard to accomplish a goal but were unable to achieve it. How did you feel?

ALSO PUBLISHED BY STONE ARCH BOOKS

DON'T GO
IN THE
CELLAR
BY JEREMY STRONG
STONE ARCH

Don't Go in the Cellar
by Jeremy Strong
1-59889-002-6

Zack finds a warning in his bedroom that tells him not to go down to the cellar. When Laura comes to visit, they go exploring — with disastrous results!

GET THAT GHOST
TO GO!
BY C. MACPHAIL
STONE ARCH

Get That Ghost to Go!
by C. MacPhail
1-59889-004-2

Duncan's life is turned upside down when Dean's ghost begins to follow him everywhere.

The
Green Men
of Gressingham
by Philip Ardagh
Author of the
EDDIE DICKENS TRILOGY
STONE ARCH

The Green Men of Gressingham
by Philip Ardagh
1-59889-000-X

The Green Men of Gressingham are medieval outlaws. When a new tax is introduced, they turn to kidnapping!

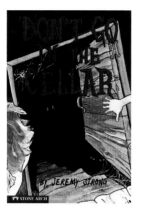

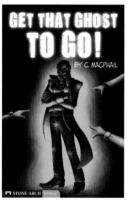

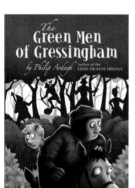

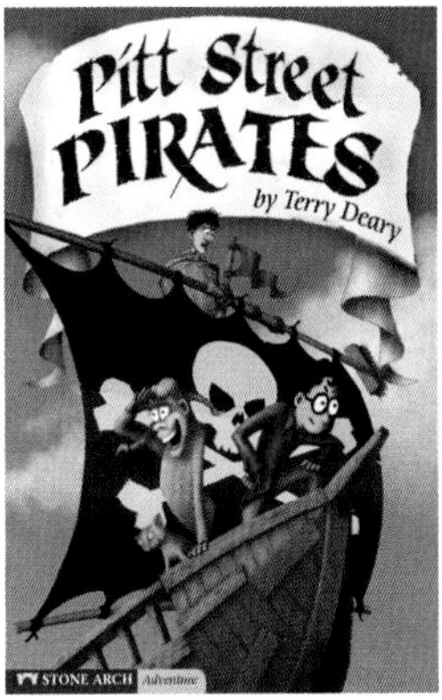
Pitt Street
PIRATES
by Terry Deary
STONE ARCH

Pitt Street Pirates

by Terry Deary

1-59889-005-0

Will these modern-day pirates be able to outwit the spoiled rich kids?

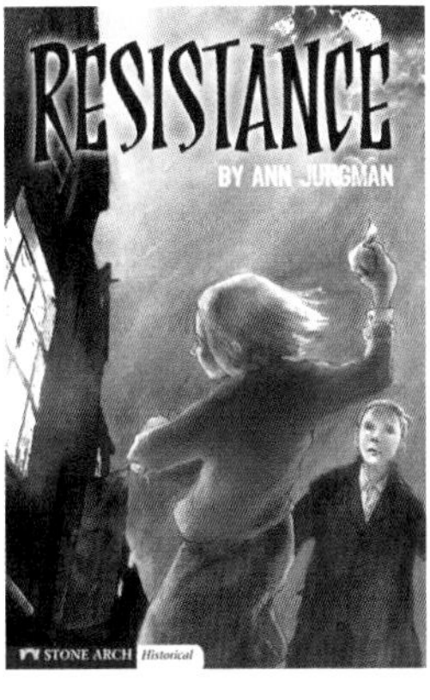
RESISTANCE
BY ANN JUNGMAN
STONE ARCH Historical

Resistance

by Ann Jungman

1-59889-001-8

Jan is ashamed when his father sides with the Germans during World War II. Can he and his best friend secretly help the Resistance?

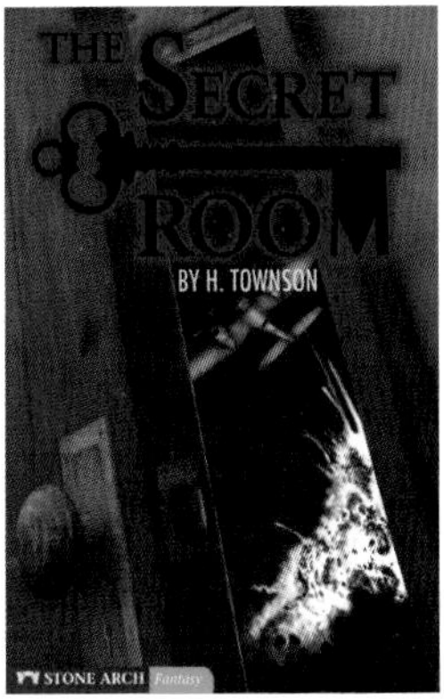
THE SECRET ROOM
BY H. TOWNSON
STONE ARCH

The Secret Room

by H. Townson

1-59889-003-4

Adam suddenly finds himself in a very different world, one in which he could be in terrible danger.

ALSO BY MICHAEL HARDCASTLE

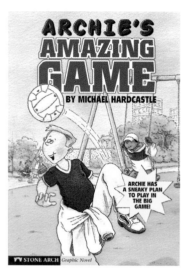

ARCHIE'S
AMAZING
GAME
BY MICHAEL HARDCASTLE
ARCHIE HAS A SNEAKY PLAN TO PLAY IN THE BIG GAME!
STONE ARCH Graphic Novel

Archie's Amazing Game
1-59889-025-5

Archie's a future soccer star, but his mother has banned him from playing during their vacation. Can he convince his siblings and friends to help him get his mom to lift the ban before the upcoming tournament?

ORDER NOW!

STONE ARCH BOOKS,
151 Good Counsel Hill Drive, Mankato, MN 56001
1-800-421-7731
www.stonearchbooks.com